ONE NIGHT TO REMEMBER

ERICA RIDLEY

ISBN: 1943794448
ISBN-13: 978-1943794447
Copyright © 2019 Erica Ridley
Model Photography © PeriodImages
Cover Design © Teresa Spreckelmeyer

ALSO BY ERICA RIDLEY

The *Wicked Dukes Club*:
One Night for Seduction by Erica Ridley
One Night of Surrender by Darcy Burke
One Night of Passion by Erica Ridley
One Night of Scandal by Darcy Burke
One Night to Remember by Erica Ridley
One Night of Temptation by Darcy Burke

Rogues to Riches:
Lord of Chance
Lord of Pleasure
Lord of Night
Lord of Temptation
Lord of Secrets
Lord of Vice

The *Dukes of War*:
The Viscount's Tempting Minx
The Earl's Defiant Wallflower
The Captain's Bluestocking Mistress
The Major's Faux Fiancée
The Brigadier's Runaway Bride
The Pirate's Tempting Stowaway

The Duke's Accidental Wife

The *12 Dukes of Christmas*:
Once Upon a Duke

Kiss of a Duke

Wish Upon a Duke

Never Say Duke

Dukes, Actually

The Duke's Bride

The Duke's Embrace

The Duke's Desire

Dawn With a Duke

One Night With a Duke

Ten Days With a Duke

Forever Your Duke

*L*ady Felicity Sutton could not stop herself from plucking yet another glass of lemonade from the tray of a passing footman. Her brother had reminded her multiple times that tonight's mission was to enchant one of the unwed lordlings wending their way about the ballroom before her. She was supposed to be on the hunt for dukes and marquesses, not sweet, delicious lemonade.

Yet no matter how many soirées she attended, or how fine the orchestra played for the dancers, a large part of Felicity could never forget how things had been *before*. Back when there were no new clothes, much less fancy gowns. Back when the siblings' only society was each other. Back when the cost of sugar or lemons was so dear, the idea of lemonade was just another unobtainable dream.

Even more than the chandeliers overhead and the elegant revelers surrounding her, nothing reminded her how far they'd come quite like the simple luxury of cold, tart-sweet lemonade any time she wished.

"No wool-gathering," her brother, now the Duke of Colehaven, murmured into her ear. "Concentrate on *earl*-gathering. You need to marry well."

"I know," she assured him. "I'm planning my attack."

Cole's relief was obvious. "Tonight's the night?"

"This Season is the Season."

She hoped. Catching a man's eye was one thing. Convincing the right man to the altar was another.

"I'll leave you to it." Cole ceased scolding her like a mother hen and threaded his way back across the ballroom toward his new wife.

Felicity shook her head fondly. There was nothing she wouldn't do for her brother, and nothing he wouldn't do for her.

It had been the two of them against the world since as far back as she could remember. Back then, he had been Caleb, and she had more often than not been "Felix." Now she was Lady Felicity and he was the Duke of Colehaven.

A few short months ago, Cole had fallen in love and taken a wife. He had never been happier, and he wanted the same happiness for his sister. In the form of a duke, ideally. Or, he supposed, an earl, if she absolutely must lower her sights. She'd had *six Seasons*. The horror! Surely it was time to make a choice.

She strode into the retiring room and made her way to one of the free spaces before the Barkleys' grand, gilt-edged looking-glass. A mahogany table placed just beneath the edge of the frame brimmed with all the accoutrements a lady exhausted by dancing might require.

Rosewater to reduce the puffiness beneath one's eyes, spare pins for one's hair, squares of cloth to dip in a bowl of iced water and press against the back of one's heated neck. Felicity loved all of it. Other ladies might take such luxuries for granted, but the scent of rosewater or the relief of a cold compress against her neck never failed to make her feel like a princess in a fairy tale.

"I fear I shall vomit," whispered an ashen debutante to Felicity's left, followed by a panicked cry of distress. "Oh dear, I *promised* I wouldn't say 'vomit' at the party! I'm not sick, I'm just… *hopeless*."

Felicity turned to the young woman with a smile. "How do you do? I'm Lady Felicity Sutton."

The girl grew even paler. "I said 'vomit' in front of the Duke of Colehaven's sister?" The young lady buried her face in her hands. "I'm ruined."

"None of that," Felicity said with amusement. "I'm not so missish, and besides, if you would like to know a secret… titled people vomit, too. But *you* won't, will you? Not in that pretty white gown. You look lovely. I imagine your dance card was filled in seconds."

"Almost," the girl admitted. She gave Felicity an abashed smile. "Thank you for being so kind. I'm Alexandra Corning. This is my first Season."

Felicity returned her smile. "Every lady present here tonight has had a first Season. You'll get used to it."

"Not *too* used to it, I hope," Miss Corning said fervently. "I daren't become a *spinster*."

The hushed word was spoken in the same tone as one might say *leper* or *pariah* or *worthless* or *doomed*.

Felicity did not blame Miss Corning for being dramatic. Most marriageable young ladies tended to share that view. Indeed, Felicity's four-and-twenty years were the reason why her brother despaired of her ever bringing a suitor up to scratch. Felicity had nothing against dukes and earls, but she wanted something *more* than luxury and a title and wealth.

She wanted to *share* the riches.

It wasn't enough to provide for her children and her children's children. She needed to do everything within her power to improve the lives of the countless impoverished children out in the streets and in the rookeries, struggling to get through each day. Children like she and Cole had once been. Children who desperately needed someone to care about them.

"Don't worry about becoming a spinster," she told Miss Corning. "Try to relax."

"I can't," Miss Corning said miserably. "My parents expect perfection."

"Everyone has a different definition of 'perfect,'" Felicity responded.

It had taken every minute of her six Seasons to find a man who fit Cole's requirements *and* hers.

To most men, Felicity's dowry alone was reason to wed her. The key was finding a man who didn't *need* it. Someone whose own fortune was vast enough that Felicity's dowry would be a sweet, if unnecessary, gesture.

Lord Raymore fit the bill perfectly.

He was not a duke, but a marquess—and two decades older—but even Cole could find no other flaws. Raymore was dizzyingly wealthy. Three of his six properties were entailed to the title, meaning no one could ever take their home away. Neither Felicity nor her children need ever fear a future living on the streets. But grand possessions weren't enough.

What was the point of marrying privilege and power if she couldn't use any of it to help the people who needed it most?

"When I'm married," Miss Corning said with a sigh, "I'll never have to lift a finger again. My husband will take care of everything."

He certainly would if she let him.

Felicity had coaxed Cole into placing "permission for wife to contribute to charitable causes as she sees fit" in her betrothal contract, but neither of them had been able to persuade any of her suitors over the years to sign such a statement.

Men control money, some insisted. *Every penny of it.* Others were happy to give her a bottomless purse, with the stipulation that her husband's money was only to be spent on accoutrements that improved the family image: jewels, elaborate gowns. Under no circumstances was she to waste their assets on other people.

"Do you have your eye on anyone in particular?" Felicity asked.

"My eye is on every man with a title," Miss Corning replied with a little laugh. "Just like everyone else."

Felicity wasn't "everyone else." Neither was Lord Raymore.

Not only was the older gentleman on the House of Lords' committee to reform child labor, he and Cole were the *only* peers on that committee. Raymore was the one bachelor in this ballroom who would be delighted to wed a bride who shared his passion to improve the lives of the less fortunate.

And in less than an hour, Felicity's hand was promised to the marquess in a waltz.

It was a good sign, but a would-be bride required more than signs. Lord Raymore danced with Felicity regularly enough to raise eyebrows, but never sought her company outside of a ballroom. If she intended to change that, she needed to look and act the part of a future marchioness.

"Your dress is beautiful," Miss Corning said shyly. "I love the tiny rosebuds on your demi-train."

"Thank you," Felicity answered with pride. The selection hadn't been easy.

She'd spent countless hours poring over fashion plates to find exactly the right styles to communicate the impression she was hoping to make.

More mature than blushing, fresh-from-the-schoolroom girls, but young enough to still be a fine catch for any discerning gentleman. Intelligent enough to run any household, yet not so managing or bossy as to be tiresome. Elegant, not gaudy. Attractive, not bawdy.

Duchess, not *desperate*.

It was a very fine line. Then again, controlling her outward appearance had been the sole tool in Felicity's arsenal for most of her life. She had always had to pretend to be someone else in order to be seen, or to get what she needed. It no longer felt like giving up part of herself.

She straightened her bodice. The right clothes made her feel safe. They let her be—or at least appear to be—whatever she chose. Before her brother had inherited a title, the boys' clothes she donned determined whether she would be accepted. Whether she would eat. Whether she could stay with her brother.

Now that Cole was a duke... nothing had changed. Her ability to mimic the right look would determine the rest of her life.

She understood exactly why a debutante like Miss Corning felt like she might vomit. Lord Raymore *had* to be the one. He was the only hope she had left.

Felicity squared her shoulders in determination. This was the night she'd be on her way to her own happy ending.

Miss Corning's shoulders slumped as she stared into the looking-glass. "My hair is hopeless."

"This will help." Using pins from the provided dish, Felicity rearranged Miss Corning's flyaway locks into a style she'd seen in *La Belle Assemblée*. She and her lady's maid had practiced this look a hundred times. Just one more pin, and... "There."

Miss Corning let out a shaky breath. "It looks beautiful. Thank you so much. I suppose I'm now as primped as I'll ever be."

"You look stunning," Felicity assured her. "Are you enjoying the ball?"

"It feels like every minuet is my one and only chance with each gentleman." Miss Corning blushed. "It must be lovely to be the sister of a duke, and not have to worry about such things."

Felicity hadn't always been the sister of a duke, and she had never stopped worrying about things.

"Come along," she told Miss Corning with what she hoped was a confident smile. "Let's return to the dancing, shall we? Perhaps we'll fill the rest of your card while we wait for the next set to begin."

Miss Corning nodded. She stuck to Felicity's side as they exited the retiring room and returned to the loud, bright whirl of the ballroom.

"There's my mother," Miss Corning said. "Oh dear, she looks vexed. Did I tarry too long?"

"Go to her," Felicity said. "Vexed or not, mothers are a precious thing to cherish."

She could not even remember hers.

"Thank you for everything." Miss Corning curtsied and hurried off.

Felicity made her way toward her acquaintance Hester Donnell.

Like Felicity, this was not Hester's first Season. Unlike Felicity, Hester had been born into this world. She did not have to pretend to belong or worry about being unmasked as inferior. To Hester, all of this grandeur was normal.

More importantly, Hester was a leader of fashion. Their amicable association had eased Felicity's entrée into Society back when Felicity had made her debut. For that, Felicity would always be grateful.

"Did you try the lemon tarts?" Hester asked as she approached.

"You know I tried the lemon tarts," Felicity responded. "I tried all the lemon tarts. I would have cleaned up the lemon tart crumbs, too, had I not been forcibly restrained by eagle-eyed footmen."

Hester smirked. "I wish that were true. A little lemon tart drama would liven up this soirée."

Even after years of running into each other at ballrooms just like this one, Felicity still struggled to understand how other people could *tire* of being surrounded by so much beauty and riches and food and music.

"How are you managing to pass the time?" she asked dryly.

Hester tilted the edge of her painted fan toward a well-dressed couple locking elbows in a country-dance. "I'm watching Penelope Wakefield captivate the Earl of Findon. Some say his eye wanders too much for him to select a bride, but he has saved a dance for Lady Penelope at least once a fortnight.

Mark my words, that man is thinking of marriage."

Felicity certainly hoped so. Not because she had any insight into whatever designs Penelope and the earl might or might not have for each other. But because Felicity and Lord Raymore had also shared a set every single week this Season, without fail.

If fortnightly attentions meant a proposal was forthcoming for Lady Penelope, surely a weekly waltz or minuet strongly indicated Lord Raymore's matrimonial intentions toward Felicity. She just needed to coax him to take the next step.

"When do you think he'll ask for her hand?" she murmured.

"Any day now," Hester replied with confidence. "Next year at this time, they'll be the hosts of the Season's biggest crush." She swirled an inch of golden liquid in her glass and muttered, "I hope they'll have better sherry."

Felicity made no response. She thought the refreshments perfectly delicious, and tonight's party positively brilliant.

"I'm rarely caught off guard in such matters," Hester continued. "I knew Lady Diana was meant for your brother the first time I saw them together."

Felicity frowned. "Did they even dance together before they were wed?"

"They did not," Hester said with portent,

"and he wanted to. Of course they were destined to marry. Everyone wants who they cannot have."

Felicity's stomach clenched. Was there some truth to what Hester was saying? Was the real reason Lord Raymore had yet to ask for Felicity's hand because she said *yes* to every dance instead of limiting her availability?

She gritted her teeth in frustration. Courtship rules were so arbitrary! Why must it be a game of winners and losers instead of frank conversations where everyone simply said exactly what they meant?

I like you.

I like you, too.

Let's get married.

Wouldn't that be much easier than making the proper hand signs to flirt with one's fan, whilst rationing out minuets and pinching one's cheeks in the retiring room between each set in order to keep up the appearance of a youthful glow?

"The expression on your face," Hester said with a laugh. "It's as if you just tried the Barkleys' dreadful sherry for the first time. What on earth are you thinking about?"

"Marriage," Felicity replied honestly.

"Believe me," Hester said, lowering her voice. "If there was a better crop to choose from, I would introduce you. I'm afraid this is it. You're looking at the best of the best."

Felicity nodded. "I know."

The truth was, marrying *anyone* in this ballroom would have seemed like a dream come true to the eight-year-old version of herself. Even being the wife of a footman would have been unthinkable. For most of her childhood, Felicity hadn't belonged anywhere. She and Cole had been lucky enough not to be alone, but love couldn't fill one's belly.

Because she and her brother weren't a part of the original duke and heirs' lives, there was little to no gossip about the dark years before Cole inherited. The people in this ballroom did not know the truth about their past, and God willing, they never would.

Felicity wasn't ashamed of anything she'd done to survive, but the truth would make her an outcast right when she was closest to finally being *in*.

That was, if she could bring Lord Raymore up to scratch.

Hester raised her brows. "I don't think you have to worry about marriage anymore."

Because of the marquess? Felicity perked up. Perhaps Hester had heard something interesting.

"What do you mean?" she asked carefully.

"You must know by now," Hester said in surprise. "This is your fifth Season."

Felicity swallowed. "Sixth."

"Exactly," Hester said dryly and returned her gaze to the dance floor.

Felicity's stomach twisted. Hester wasn't suggesting a marriage proposal was on the horizon. She was saying it was *too late*.

"I'm four-and-twenty," she whispered.

"Mm-hmm," Hester said absently. "I'm almost two-and-twenty. This is my last year."

Felicity drew back in horror. "Two-and-twenty is *not* the end!"

"Oh, of course not," Hester agreed. "Not for me. I've always known who I'll marry. Our fathers made a pact when we were children. Titus and I made our own pact to enjoy three Seasons of independence before joining in marriage. He's got the license. We'll marry next month."

Felicity stared at her before managing a faint, "Congratulations."

She'd known she was tempting the devil by waiting this long to marry, but she hadn't considered the possibility that things were already *dire*. Felicity's chest tightened. She'd promised her brother she'd be betrothed before the end of the Season. She promised herself she'd make measurable progress with Lord Raymore before the end of the night.

This was her best opportunity.

The orchestra lowered their bows and dancers dispersed from the polished floor. One of the gentlemen made his way in their direction. Tall, sandy hair, dark eyes... the Earl of Thistlebury.

Felicity straightened. She had one more set

free before her promised dance with Lord Raymore.

The earl bowed to them both before extending his elbow toward Hester. "I believe this is my dance?"

Hester winked at Felicity over his shoulder as if to imply she was very much enjoying her last month of freedom.

Felicity wished she were enjoying the evening, too. Not standing around awkwardly next to an empty spot where her already betrothed friend had just waltzed off with an earl.

She accepted a glass of sherry from a passing footman just to have something to do with her hands.

Out of habit, she scanned the ballroom for Lord Raymore. Theirs was the following set. Felicity would not be so forward as to approach him before it was time, but she *was* standing about with a cup of delicious, allegedly subpar sherry, and it wouldn't hurt to have someone to converse with.

There. Lord Raymore's shock of salt-and-pepper hair caught her eye.

The marquess was *not* standing about with no company save for a glass of sherry in one hand. He was in the center of the dance floor, enjoying a minuet with none other than Miss Corning.

The shy debutante was gazing up at the marquess with high color on the apples of her youthful cheeks, her hair resplendent in the style Felicity had crafted with her bare hands.

Wonderful.

Felicity set her unfinished sherry behind a potted plant. All was not lost, but she needed a clear mind when she danced with Lord Raymore if she wished to have any hope of impressing him as a better option than the blushing cherub currently in his arms.

Quickly, she circumnavigated the dance floor toward her brother and his wife, careful not to stray too near to the dancers. The last thing Felicity needed was for Lord Raymore to catch sight of her alone and partnerless, and develop second thoughts about his own interest.

When she reached her brother and his wife, they were no longer alone.

Arrogant blowhard Silas Wiltchurch was bending Cole's ear on some matter or another. Wiltchurch was the nephew of one of the patronesses of Almack's. No matter how unbearable he might be, no one dared gainsay him unless they wished to be barred for life. Wiltchurch never let anyone forget the danger of crossing him.

"Am I interrupting something important?" Felicity asked her sister-in-law in a low voice.

Diana rolled her eyes. "Racing is not important. Interrupt all you like."

Felicity returned Diana's smile, but her interest was piqued. *Racing* might not be important to Diana, but it interested Felicity very much indeed. Particularly if the race in question involved mechanical conveyances. The only thing Felicity loved more than horses were carriages.

"What are we racing?" she asked lightly.

Before Cole could reply, Silas Wiltchurch let out a huff. "*You* are not racing anything. Ladies do not race. *We* means Colehaven and me, and a few other *men*."

Cole turned to Felicity as if Wiltchurch had not spoken. "Carriages. Curricles, specifically. You might be interested to know that—"

She shook her head slightly before he could continue.

Although she knew her brother would never say anything truly scandalous—like, *I'll be racing the carriage you modified for me*—Silas Wiltchurch was right.

Even the most superficial interest in "manly matters" displayed on her part might be enough to dissuade a conservative older gentleman like Lord Raymore from considering her as a future bride. She could not take the risk.

Unfortunately, Wiltchurch had noticed Felicity's little shake of the head.

"Ohhh," he said with exaggerated impatience. "First you interrupt a conversation that has nothing to do with you to ask what it's about, and then you attempt to silence us when your brother tries to answer your impertinent question." He turned back to Cole. "It's not your fault. Inferior female brains aren't capable of comprehending anything more substantial than ostrich feathers and French lace."

Cole looked like he was about to put his fist through Wiltchurch's face.

"You're so right." Felicity infused her voice with cloying saccharine, hoping to diffuse the tension before she drew all the wrong sort of attention. She gave her brother a pointed look. "Ladies rarely even enter a carriage without the aid of a gentleman. What could we possibly know about the art of racing one?"

"Precisely." His pride restored, Wiltchurch turned his back to Felicity and resumed his conversation as if he had never noticed her arrival.

"Insufferable prig," she muttered beneath her breath.

Diana grinned in solidarity. "He wouldn't recognize sarcasm if it hit him."

"I thought *Cole* was going to hit him," Felicity admitted.

"He was definitely going to hit him," Diana assured her. "And I was going to let him."

"My peacekeeping will haunt me to my dying day," Felicity said with a sigh.

Diana's eyes twinkled. "We both know which one of them owns the superior curricle… and why."

The thought should have warmed Felicity's heart. Diana's inclusion into the family had doubled the number of people who knew Felicity's secret.

Today, it just made her sad.

She was *tired* of having to hide her mechanical capabilities. Tired of having to pretend she was too clueless to follow along, too "proper" to be part of the conversation.

Her brother didn't miss the old days. Felicity... well, she didn't miss the hunger pangs or the cold nights or the endless uncertainty, but the day that the more knowledgeable lads at the forge stopped seeing her as a worthless hanger-on and started treating her as an equal?

Of course she missed that.

For a moment, what she wanted most was not to blend in with the other ladies, but to challenge Silas Wiltchurch to a curricle race in front of all and sundry. She could beat a slug like him blindfolded.

But she would never have the chance.

"Snare your big fish yet?" Diana asked, meaning Lord Raymore.

"Next set," Felicity murmured back. "God willing."

She was grateful down to her bones for every advantage she possessed, and she knew what she had to do to keep it.

Was she scared of poverty? *Terrified.* She'd been frightened and miserable every day of her childhood and would never risk her offspring experiencing such a fate.

But marrying the marquess was far more than a way to ensure her personal security, or even her children's futures. Felicity did not want *any* child to go through the hell she and her brother had. It wasn't living. It was barely surviving. And even so, others hadn't been so lucky.

Marrying well wasn't just for her. It was for everyone who didn't have a way out. The better Felicity was set up, the more she could help others. *That* was worth any sacrifice.

The first act she intended to take as Lady Raymore was to sponsor opportunities and housing for homeless or impoverished children like she and her brother once were. Cole donated handsomely, but he was one person. Felicity and her husband would be two more. Hester Donnell had agreed to support Felicity's future foundation, and spread the word to her friends as well. With luck and hard work, Felicity and her powerful husband could start a movement.

It might be impossible to save *all* the children, but she would bloody well die trying.

Even if it meant putting up with unconscionable self-important prigs like Silas Wiltchurch.

"Thank God," Diana muttered when Wiltchurch at last flounced away. "I got tired of not throttling him."

"Agreed," Felicity said with feeling, then turned to her brother. "When's the big race?"

"*Never*," Diana interrupted before Cole could reply. "I don't trust Wiltchurch as far as I can throw him, and believe me, I'd very much like to throw him. Let him race other madmen. I want you to stay in one piece."

"I already gave my word as a gentleman," Cole protested. "Last night at the Wicked Duke, I was boasting about the curricle that a certain master mechanic has been conditioning for me—"

"You're welcome," Felicity murmured.

"—and the next thing I knew, six of us were scheduled for a curricle race at dawn, two weeks from Saturday."

"It's like you can't hear me," Diana said. "Allow me to summarize. The key word was 'No.'"

"I heard you," Cole assured her. "And I have the perfect solution. My *carriage* is obliged to present itself at Hyde Park on the appointed hour, but *I* am not required to be the man at the reins. The Curricle King does this sort of thing all the time. I'm certain he'll be delighted to thrash Silas Wiltchurch yet again."

Felicity's heart skipped. The "Curricle King" was Giles Langford.

Talented and clever, reckless and dangerous, Langford was a notorious whip and a god among coach smiths. There were rumors that women with dampened bodices crowded Hyde Park at dawn to glimpse the handsome daredevil winning another race, only to swoon at the mere sight of him.

Not proper ladies, of course. Much as she wished to, Felicity had never laid eyes on the Curricle King. Nonetheless, his reputation spoke for itself.

"Langford could win with one hand tied behind his back," she agreed in satisfaction. "With him as your driver and me as your—"

"I believe this is my dance?" came a bemused voice from just behind her.

Felicity whirled around to see Lord Raymore patiently waiting with one arm extended… and the rest of the dance floor already filled with new couples.

"Of course," she stammered.

Her face heated as she took his arm. Had she really almost said *with me as your mechanic* out loud in the middle of a ballroom? Good God. She had to do better than that.

She took a deep, calming breath as Raymore led her to join the others for the first waltz of the evening. This Season might be her last opportunity. She had to do everything right.

"Thank you for this dance," she murmured.

The marquess smiled. "I always enjoy dancing with you."

That was something, wasn't it? A step in the right direction.

The problem was, they'd been making the same rhythmic steps once a week all Season long. They needed to see each other outside of the occasional ballroom if their courtship had any hope of blossoming into marriage.

He wasn't Felicity's best chance. He was her *only* chance.

If it meant hinting at her willingness to turn their weekly half-hour intervals into something more substantial, then so be it.

She peered up at him through her lashes and offered her sweetest, most biddable smile.

"I always look forward to sharing a set with you," she responded. "I'd be amenable to seeing each other more often. If the weather holds tomorrow, it should be a lovely day to enjoy the park."

There. Forward, but hopefully not *too* forward. In any case, the words were out. Where they took them was up to Lord Raymore.

"Oh," the marquess said with an embarrassed wince. "Not tomorrow, I'm afraid. I've promised to take Miss Corning for ices, and then a visit to the theatre."

Ices.

A public appearance in Raymore's theatre box.

Young, pretty, first-Season-debutante Miss Corning. Not Felicity. Her stomach sank.

"Of course," she murmured. "I understand."

There went the one man who could provide everything she dreamed.

CHAPTER 2

Giles Langford whistled a jaunty Irish melody as he organized the tools hanging from nails or arranged on shelves strategically placed about his shop. Although he held a soft spot for all smithies, his favorite would always be his own. He grew up here, in this very chamber, at his father's knee learning everything he could.

Friends and customers alike often teased him about owning the cleanest smithy in all of England. He ignored their jests. Not only was Giles fond of *a place for everything and everything in its place,* but he would also always consider this space to belong to both him and his father alike. He would never disrespect his father by failing to take care of something the family owned.

When the smithy was tidied to his liking, Giles crossed over to Baby, the much-loved lightweight conveyance in the center. His father had helped him build this curricle. They'd begun with nothing more than a dream and ended with a thing of beauty, built with their own hands.

That was, until the tremors and involuntary movements started. When Father could no longer keep any tools clutched in his shaking grasp, he'd been forced to watch without participating. He swore it gave him just as much pride to witness everything his son could accomplish on his own.

It had taken Giles much longer to get used to working without his father.

But he didn't work alone. A smithy this busy required talented journeymen to helm each specialized post. Giles also sponsored close to a dozen apprentices; some in the traditional manner, and some… less so.

He raked a final glance over a small table prepared with two pitchers of fresh lemonade and checked his pocket watch. If prior history was any indication, every drop would be gone within the next half an hour.

"Mr. Langford! Mr. Langford!" The shouts were accompanied by the patter of a dozen boots rushing into the smithy at once.

Giles gave a welcoming smile to his six young charges, then motioned to what they *really* wanted—the lemonade in the corner.

As they crossed the threshold into the smithy, the six lads ceased elbowing each other and assumed the exaggeratedly calm mien of the responsible, mature blacksmith apprentices they hoped to someday be.

Most of the children who spent time in the Langford smithy lived nearby, although a few came from the neighboring rookery St. Giles. His good friend Hugh Tarleton was a rector of a local church, and occasionally dropped off a lad who needed something to do with his time besides make trouble.

Although Tarleton often teased the children that they were in the presence of the modern-day Saint Giles for "rescuing" so many of their brethren, Giles didn't feel particularly saintly. He and the children were helping each other.

As business increased and Giles expanded the smithy to include the properties on either side, there was room for more carriages, more horses—and more apprentices. Including the neighborhood lads had been a natural extension. Welcoming a few more from Tarleton's church was no hardship at all. Giles enjoyed the company.

That his charges were every creed and color only made them more delightful. The boys didn't bond over shared backgrounds. They bonded because for once, they all believed in their future.

After consuming every drop of lemonade in the pitchers, the lads wiped their upper lips and assumed their posts shadowing their assigned journeymen. Giles could not hide his fondness of the six bright-eyed children their neighborhood had previously given up on.

He glanced up at the sight of a carriage halting just outside the open doors of the smithy. When he caught sight of the ducal crest upon the door, Giles strode outside to attend to the visitor himself.

The door opened to reveal one of the Duke of Colehaven's footmen.

"Harris," Giles said warmly. "How have you been?"

"Very well, Mr. Langford." The footman stepped down from the carriage. "And yourself?"

"Can't complain," Giles answered.

It was true. Business was booming, with every year even more successful than the last. Only a sentimental fool would grumble because he had no partner to share it with.

The sign overhead read *Langford*, just as it had done for thirty years. Father had promised to repaint it *Langford & Langford* once Giles commissioned his first paying client on his own, thereby proving himself worthy of becoming a full partner. Then the tremors started. Giles became the only Langford in the smithy long before either of them were ready.

He didn't need a partner, Giles reminded himself. The past fifteen years had proved that. He had done far more than commission a single paying client. The smithy was now flanked by his large carriage house and full mews, and had become as revered for some people as Vauxhall Gardens or Kensington Palace.

To have accomplished all that as a solitary Langford should make him proud, not sad.

"How can I be of service?" he asked Harris.

The footman handed him a folded square of paper bearing a wax seal. "Message from His Grace. He would appreciate your immediate reply."

Giles accepted the letter. The Duke of Colehaven was one of the smithy's most important clients. They had met ten years ago this spring, when His Grace and a cohort had formed the Wicked Duke tavern near the Haymarket and opened its doors to any man, regardless of background or status.

Seeing an opportunity to expand his client list into the lucrative world of the ton, Giles had forged some items for Colehaven for free, in order to prove the speed and quality of his work. The gamble paid off. With the vocal support of a young, popular duke, the cachet of being one of Giles's valued clients exploded overnight.

Whatever favor was requested inside the folded missive, Giles would see to it at once. Although His Grace might not realize it, Colehaven had rescued the Langford smithy when it teetered on the precipice of failure. A debt like that could never fully be repaid.

He broke the seal without further ado.

Langford,

In a fortnight, my curricle must win a race. I realize I am scarcely giving an hour's notice, but please let my man know if you can pay my carriage house a visit this afternoon at four o'clock for a quick inspection of the vehicle.

Colehaven

"*Please.*" That was another way Colehaven was different from other peers. His Grace never failed to treat Giles as though a coach smith's time was just as valuable as his own.

"Of course." Giles refolded the letter. "Please let His Grace know I will present myself at his carriage house by four o'clock as requested."

"Right away." Harris disappeared without delay.

Giles turned back toward his smithy and paused. His journeymen and their studious apprentices were busy at their posts. Colehaven was one of their most valued clients. Since Giles was not needed in the smithy at the moment, was there any reason to make His Grace wait?

Bunyan, the duke's stablemaster, was a jolly, friendly fellow, and had been an associate of Giles's father long before the current duke had inherited the title. It would be splendid to see the irreverent old codger again.

In the interest of speed, Giles took a horse rather than a carriage, and made his way to Grosvenor Square. He tied his horse to a post along the narrow cobblestone lane behind the town house and headed toward the open carriage doors at the rear.

"Good afternoon," he called out as he approached.

Although no one came to greet him, the sound of scurrying feet indicated his presence had caused some sort of stir.

"Are you certain?" whispered a youthful voice from behind the closest carriage.

"Positive," an excited voice whispered back. "I swear it's the Curricle King. He's been here before."

Giles hid his grin and pretended he hadn't overheard. "Good afternoon, lads. Is Bunyan about?"

Three boys stepped out from behind the carriage with flushed cheeks and wide eyes.

"B-Bunyan?" stammered one.

"We expect 'im in an hour," said the other.

So much for offering prompt service by arriving early to his appointment. Now that Giles was here, however, going home just to turn around and come back would be a ridiculous waste of his time. He might as well glance over the carriage in order to have his report ready for Bunyan when the man arrived at four.

"I'm here to inspect the curricle," he informed the stable boys. "Do you mind if I get started?"

The lads exchanged doubtful looks.

Belatedly, Giles recalled that Colehaven was unusually fussy about meetings being held at precisely their appointed hour. An odd trait, given that half the ton were barely rising from slumber at three in the afternoon, much less worrying about keeping appointments to the very minute.

"The c-curricle?" asked one of the lads. "Not the coach?"

"The curricle," Giles assured him, and pointed. "That one."

Yet the wide-eyed stable boys remained positioned between him and the ducal carriages, as if they weren't certain whether to beg for the Curricle King's autograph or bar him from entry.

Of the two outcomes, the latter would be the most surprising. This was not Giles's first visit. He could see the deuced curricle from here and had been summoned to work on it. What the devil was the problem?

"It'll only be a moment," he promised the stable boys. "I'll just have a quick once-over, to gauge whether the vehicle requires more than a routine safety inspection."

A *harrumph* sounded from elsewhere in the mews.

Giles glanced about in surprise, but saw no one other than the stable boys. He frowned. The strange sound must have been a gust of wind playing tricks.

He took a step in the direction of the duke's curricle.

All three stable boys immediately fell behind him, like ducklings paddling after their mother.

"Did you do it?" the closest stable boy asked breathlessly. "Did you truly reach the finish line before Mr. Wiltchurch even made it halfway down Rotten Row?"

Giles tamped down a satisfied smile. One did not gloat over one's racing wins, even if the losing party referred to him as "nothing more than a bloody blacksmith" or "a self-important peasant."

"I did indeed," Giles acknowledged as he strode to the duke's curricle. "Is Mr. Wiltchurch who His Grace will be racing?"

The lads nodded in unison.

His chest lightened. *Good.* Colehaven and his curricle were more than a match for a rash know-it-all like Wiltchurch. Giles pulled a wrench from his leather satchel and began to check each bolt's tightness.

The stable boys kept right on his heels.

Giles didn't mind. He had once been a green lad just like them, eager to soak up experience and wisdom. Dreaming of someday having a carriage of his own.

The maintenance on the duke's conveyances was second to none. In all the inspections Giles had performed in this carriage house, he had never once come across a loose axle or a missing bolt or an ill-seating spring or so much as a speck of rust. Every vehicle was always in impeccable condition.

Today was no exception. The duke's racing curricle was in such immaculate shape, one could be forgiven for believing it had been serviced by a master craftsman moments before Giles walked through the door.

Nonetheless, he went through all the safety points in his mental list, skipping nothing. Not a day went by without a dozen accidents clogging up the already congested streets. Safety was a coach smith's top priority.

"See this coupling?" he asked the boys as he ducked beneath to show them. "The reason we always check this one…"

The lads followed excitedly, peppering his explanations with questions and exclamations. Before long, he and the stable boys had hunched and crawled their way to the opposite side of the curricle.

Giles slipped his tools back into his leather satchel and turned toward the enthusiastic lads. "Next, let's turn our focus to the wheels, in order to have an in-depth look at—"

Shapely ankles.

He blinked and looked again.

Dainty boots. A hint of lace. And two lovely ankles. Tucked beneath a stately coach. Barely visible behind the trio of stable boys. Almost as if they'd placed themselves in just the right position to block the coach's under-carriage from view.

Almost…

As if…

Giles spun to face the lads. "There is a woman in your carriage house."

"No," the first boy said without hesitation. "Absolutely not."

The others shook their heads just as firmly. "No women here."

"There *is.*" As foolish as he felt saying so, Giles could not refute the evidence before his eyes. Ladies' half-boots, feminine ankles, lace trim attached to what appeared to be delicate pantalettes. It did not require a Bow Street in-spector to put these clues together. He pointed between their shoulders. "Look there! A woman is hiding beneath the duke's pri-mary coach."

The lads glanced at each other before shaking their heads with even more fervor. "No females allowed here, sir."

Giles frowned. If the lads were hiding her, then she must not have permission to be present. Which meant what? Twelve-year-old stable boys were colluding with some madwoman bent on… theft? Sabotage? Not on Giles's watch.

"Then what the devil is she doing beneath the carriage?" He pushed past the lads and dropped to his haunches beside the coach.

From this angle, he could not glimpse her face.

"Come out of there," he ordered.

She did not move.

Giles narrowed his eyes over his shoulder at the three white-faced lads. "If the Duke of Colehaven finds out you've allowed a stranger to infiltrate his carriage house…"

All three boys blushed in unison.

"Not a stranger," spluttered one.

"He already knows," blurted another.

"Oh, for the love of…" With a breathtakingly unladylike muttered curse, the owner of the shapely ankles and lacy pantalettes wriggled out from beneath the Duke of Colehaven's family coach.

Striking dark eyes glared out at him from a beautiful heart-shaped face. Silky coils of dark brown hair dipped from a crooked, oil-stained mobcap. Her well-tailored dress might have been the equal of any day gown belonging to the Quality…were it not for its horrifically frayed hems, unpatched holes, and impressive collection of enough grease stains to hide whatever had once been the fabric's intended pattern.

One dusty hand clutched the neck of a

worn leather satchel not unlike Giles's own. In her other ungloved hand was a large iron wrench.

From the expression on her face, she was as prepared to wield it as a weapon as she was to use it as a tool.

Had he thought her presence mysterious before? She was now a full-blown enigma.

"Who *are* you?" he breathed.

"Stable lass," she said briskly, as if those two words came close to resolving all his unanswered questions.

"Stable lass?" he repeated, tasting the unfamiliar words as they tripped from his tongue.

"Easy to understand. Stable *lads*..." She pointed at the three boys with the end of her wrench, then turned it toward her chest. "Stable *lass*. There. We've met. Good day."

"I..." He turned to the lads, half-expecting to hear a chorus of protesting *No, definitely not, no stable lasses here, sir.*

Instead, they stared back at him wide-eyed and pasty-cheeked, as if their deepest, most heartfelt wish was that they'd never allowed him to inspect their master's curricle after all.

Giles turned back to Stable Lass. If this was her place of employment, then he had no business interfering with her work. Then again, if this was her place of employment, the stable boys would have had no reason to lie about her presence or her purpose.

Something was definitely up. Giles narrowed his eyes in suspicion. He valued Colehaven too much to turn a blind eye while mischief was being committed.

"Why are you here?" he asked.

She dropped her wrench back into her satchel as if she was already bored with the encounter. "Do you want to test me, O great and powerful Curricle King?"

Bloody right, he did. She was beautiful and defiant and fascinating, and he'd met her crawling out from under a carriage with a wrench in her hand. The duke had a right to know if she was trespassing.

Giles opened his mouth.

She sighed, and began to point her index finger about the carriage house. "Barouche, landau, cabriolet, coach, and modified curricle."

A fair enough parlor trick. "Many people—"

"Can name the types and styles of carriages? Very well. Let us see what pieces comprise a modern conveyance." She began demonstrating the parts of the closest barouche, from the folding calash top to each nut and washing.

Giles snapped his jaw closed. He'd seen apprentices who couldn't name half the components that comprised a carriage, much less explain the precise function of each part.

"Not enough?" asked the stable lass with faux innocence. She retrieved a hammer and

chisel from her satchel and turned to the curricle he'd been inspecting. "Let's take this one
apart, then put it back together. I'll begin with
the—"

"So you're a stable lass," Giles said in a
rush, interrupting her before the duke's prized
—and, yes, subtly modified—curricle was in a
hundred pieces on the sawdust-covered floor.

Even if such a shocking event would have
cost both of them their posts, part of Giles
wished he could have let her do so, just to
watch her work.

"Why didn't you just say you worked
here?" He tipped his hat to indicate he came in
peace and meant no harm. "I'm Giles
Langford."

She arched her brows. "I know."

He waited.

She said nothing.

He cleared his throat. "And you are…?"

"Declining to answer," she replied sweetly.

Her name was none of his business, he reminded himself. He was here to speak to
crotchety old Bunyan, not some cheeky stable
lass… who… knew every nut and bolt inside
this carriage house?

"It's *you*," he realized suddenly.

Nonchalance vanished from her eyes at
once, replacing her playful expression with
one of wariness. "What's me?"

"You're the one who has been keeping
Colehaven's carriages in impeccable condi-

tion." Bunyan was a lovely man, but he was far from spry these days. Giles had long assumed the old man had an apprentice or two. He just hadn't expected to meet her like this.

Stable Lass blinked. A tentative smile curved one edge of her dusky pink lips. "You're right. It is me."

"Can you teach my other clients to have half as much good sense?" Giles asked. "They should all hire stable lasses, if they're half as competent as you."

The smile blossomed into a grin, and the entire mews was transformed with its beauty.

"I would never dream of stealing work from the Curricle King," she assured him with a sassy smile, then ducked out of sight behind the coach.

He ignored the impulse to follow in her wake.

Inserting himself had been one thing when he'd believed her to be up to mischief. Giles was not foolish enough to prevent a valued employee from performing her duties. Rather than ousting a trespasser, Giles would be the one who found himself out on his ear.

If he'd met her anywhere but a client's carriage house, however… Giles shook his head. He was not in the market for a romance, here or anywhere. Besides, he'd visited this carriage house for a decade without crossing paths with Miss Lass. Another decade might pass before their paths converged again.

"Langford," came a familiar male voice from the other side of the carriage. "Good afternoon."

Colehaven! Giles turned to face his client and blinked to discover a kitten cleaving to the duke's shoulder.

"A fine afternoon, indeed. Almost as fine as your curricle." Giles gestured beside him. "I'm not certain I've been earning my keep. Every time I check on one of your carriages, it's already in great condition."

"Great isn't good enough," Colehaven replied with a remarkably straight face, given the kitten was now playfully batting his earlobe. "I need it to be the best. There's a race it needs to win."

"You're an excellent driver," Giles said honestly.

"Thank you." The duke plucked the kitten from the side of his head and settled it against his chest. "But I shan't be at the reins. I'm hoping to employ *you* for the task."

"Absolutely," Giles answered without hesitation. "And you needn't fear. I've won every race in which I oversaw my carriage."

"This time," the duke said as his kitten shredded his neckcloth, "you'll work on a team."

"A what?" Giles said blankly.

"A team," the duke repeated. "With my mechanical artisan assisting with the technical aspects and you handling the actual race, there'll be no choice but to win."

"There's no choice," Giles said, "in one important aspect at least. *I* am the carriage smith, and the man handling the reins. Therefore, *I* shall handle the technical aspects. I'll win your race, but I work alone."

"Until now," the duke agreed, and lifted the kitten from his ruined cravat. "Langford, I want you to meet your new partner."

For a single, unreal moment, Giles feared the duke was referring to his cat.

But then Stable Lass emerged from behind the duke's coach and everything tilted even more off-kilter.

Giles cleared his throat. This was a distraction he could not afford. "While I do not doubt the skill level of your lady mechanic—"

"Not 'lady mechanic,'" the duke interrupted. "Lady Felicity. My sister."

Giles blinked.

Stable Lass smiled.

"You have got to be bamming me." Giles stepped backward in disbelief. Stable Lass was the duke's *sister?*

"No bamming," the duke assured him. "In fact, there are several new rules I expect both of you to follow."

"No rules," Miss Lass—er, Lady Felicity— said at once.

Colehaven ignored the interruption. "No

one knows my carriages better than my sister."

Giles opened his mouth.

"Not even you," the duke said as the cat hung from his waistcoat by its claws. "Any concern of Felicity's, no matter how small, must be treated with prompt and thorough consideration."

Giles opened his mouth wider.

"During this temporary working relationship," the duke continued without pausing, "you are to treat her as a peer."

"Your mechanic outranks me," Giles pointed out. "She's *Lady* Felicity."

His mind still hadn't managed to grasp it.

"Not that kind of peer," Colehaven said. "*Your* peer. Her insights and intelligence should be treated with the same respect you would give the man who taught you everything you know about carriages."

"I changed my mind," Lady Felicity said. "I like your rules."

Giles did not. Even if he attempted to follow them to the letter, there was no chance of any person being equal to Giles's father. It was the real reason he refused to consider a partner. He'd never met someone whose skills deserved partnering with. Giles's fingers clenched.

He'd been working on carriages from the moment he was old enough to toddle behind his father in the family smithy. Giles lived and breathed carriages every moment of every day. It wasn't a passion. It was an obsession. A way to be extraordinary.

And after working his entire life to be the absolute best at what he did, some rich debutante expected to be his master on a whim?

He ground his teeth in frustration.

"Next." The duke turned to his sister. "Felicity."

"Don't you think those are enough rules?" she asked. "Definitely enough rules."

"Two more," Colehaven said, unsmiling. "There will be no more future projects. After this race, you must leave the smithing to the blacksmiths and high society to the society ladies."

"Meaning me," she said without rancor. "I am a society lady. You're right. That's the future I want and the only competition I should be trying to win. This race shall be my swan song."

She didn't look like a society lady. She looked like trouble. Soft dark hair, big brown eyes, heavy crowbar…

"Lastly." The duke turned toward Giles. "Because of our long relationship, I am trusting you to keep my sister's secret. If you breathe the slightest hint of the truth to anyone else, or treat her as anything other than a respected associate…" Colehaven's eyes turned deadly. "I will destroy you."

Giles jerked his shoulders back, insulted. "I

am a professional and know how to act like one, Your Grace."

"Splendid." The duke tried and failed to separate the kitten from what had once been a stylish lapel. "In exchange for your time, efforts, and unparalleled expertise with carriages, you'll receive a bank draft for one hundred pounds. And another two hundred for your permanent discretion regarding your gracious temporary partnership with my sister."

One temporary partner.

Two short weeks.

Three hundred quid.

"I agree," Giles managed. Being dictated to by his "betters" chafed. But for that amount of money, he would swallow his pride and allow them to treat him like "just some blacksmith" for the next fortnight.

Even if he hated every minute of it.

"How much did you wager?" Lady Felicity whispered to her brother.

"It's not the coin," the duke murmured back. "It's *winning*."

"You'll win," Lady Felicity assured him, then turned her sparkling gaze and plump lips toward Giles. "*We'll* win."

"I know," the duke said simply. "You two are the best. And now you're partners."

Temporary partners. Fourteen days and counting.

Giles relaxed his shoulders. "You may consult as you please, but no hands-on inter-ference."

She shook her head. "My house, my rules."

"In the *carriage* house," he said patiently, "*my* rules."

She folded her arms over her chest. "It's my carriage house."

"It's your *brother's* carriage house," he reminded her. "Your brother's horses, your brother's curricle, *my* life at stake during the race. I will personally ensure the vehicle remains in pristine working condition."

"Pristine condition isn't enough." She touched one of the axle's cast spindles with the tips of her fingers. "Cole just wants to win his wager. *I* think we can exceed everyone's expectations. If we change these skeins for—"

"You want to renovate an already perfect curricle?" Giles asked in disbelief.

She lifted her chin. "I want to innovate an even better one."

"If it doesn't work, we'd have to start over," he pointed out. "If we don't have time, we'll lose the race."

"It'll work," she insisted. As though being a lady meant anything she dreamed would automatically come true.

"It's a terrible idea," he said in a flat voice. "The answer is no."

"You two seem to have things well in hand," the duke said briskly as he opened the town house access door and vainly attempted to fling the kitten from his shoulder. "Make the magic happen."

With that, he and the kitten dangling from his collar disappeared inside.

The wide, airy carriage house suddenly seemed closed and confining, as if Giles and Lady Felicity were not in a large open chamber but rather trapped inside a tiny glass box. He swallowed. She was standing several feet away from him and still seemed close enough to touch. Too close.

He could smell a faint hint of lavender, as though she had just taken a fragrant bath before heading out to the dirty mews. He wondered if the scent came from her skin or hair, and was vehemently grateful he was not close enough to find out.

She lifted her worn leather satchel off a nail and looped the wide strap over one shoulder.

Without another word, she marched over to the curricle and, point for point, began making the same methodical inspection Giles had begun when he'd thought he was waiting on Bunyan.

Giles couldn't help it. He was impressed.

"You're very thorough," he said gruffly as he followed her through each point.

They were crouched shoulder-to-shoulder behind the curricle's single axle, ostensibly to confirm the current condition of the dumb irons and elliptic springs.

Giles accidentally also took this opportunity to confirm the lavender-scented condition of Lady Felicity's soft, dark hair.

Respected colleague, he reminded himself. The duke's threat to ruin Giles was not idle. Colehaven's support had increased the Langford smithy's popularity. Colehaven's censure could make Giles's smithy *un*fashionable just as quickly.

Lady Felicity turned her head to face him. When her eyes met his, the corners crinkled and he could swear their pretty irises twinkled, even in the shadows.

"I can't be the worst partner to have. You've said for years that Cole's carriages are always kept in the best condition you've ever seen," she told him. "You just didn't know I was the one doing it."

"Who told you I said that?" he asked in surprise. "Bunyan?"

"You did, just now." Lady Felicity didn't bother to hide her laughter.

He gave a reluctant grin in reply. She was partly right. No matter how much money her brother tossed in their direction, Giles and Lady Felicity would never be true partners, even for a fortnight.

To his surprise, however, he wondered if they might enjoy themselves a tiny bit after all.

"Does it bother you?" she asked.

He grimaced. "Working with a partner?"

"Working with *me* as your partner." She plucked at her skirts as if mortified by their presence. "A lady mechanic."

"I don't care what gender you are," he replied honestly.

Giles had spent years building a name for himself as London's premier expert. Being assigned as the pet blacksmith to some lordling's younger brother would not have stung any less.

To his horror, Lady Felicity blinked away a sudden glassiness in her eyes.

"There's no crying in carriage houses," he stammered in alarm. "Isn't that one of your brother's rules?"

"Probably." She gave him a lopsided smile. "It's just… if you don't care about my gender, that would make you the first one."

"If I had to choose a temporary partner," he informed her, "between you and your brother, I would probably choose… the cat."

A laugh startled from Lady Felicity and she shoved his shoulder with her own. "Liar."

"Caught." He pushed to his feet so he could resume a safe distance. "To be honest, it's a refreshing surprise to be with a client who actually knows what they're talking about. And yes, you're the first lady mechanical artisan I've met."

"Not for long," she muttered as she rose to her feet.

He raised his brows. Had debutantes exchanged watercolors for wrenches?

"There are more?"

"There'll be fewer," she corrected, and gestured about the carriage house. "When I marry, I'll have to give all this up and be the mistress of a grand household. There won't be time for tinkering." She bit her lip. "Not that a married lady would dirty her hands even if she did have the time. I won't have any. I'll be too busy."

"Busy being fancy?" he asked dryly.

She crossed her arms. "Fancy doesn't mean *worse*."

It also didn't mean *better*. But it was her life and her choice. He wouldn't be part of it either way.

"Let's concentrate on the carriage," he suggested. "There's no sense worrying about the future."

"All I think about is the future," she muttered.

He couldn't imagine a worse use of her time. "Are you worried about the race?"

"No." She pushed a stray curl from her forehead. "I know Cole's carriage will be the fastest. I'm worried about how my life will turn out afterward. Why? Are *you* worried about the race?"

"No." As long as he concentrated on work. "I know I'll be the fastest driver, but more importantly, the race is two weeks away. Worrying about it doesn't help anything. It's better to relax and enjoy whatever is happening right now."

He wasn't certain which one of them had stepped closer to the other—or if they had both done so—but he was suddenly very aware that her plump, rosy lips were not nearly far enough away from his.

"What *is* happening right now?" she asked softly.

A colossal distraction when he most needed to stay focused. And professional. And a much safer distance from the Duke of Colehaven's sister.

"Nothing at all is happening," he said, as much to warn himself as to remind her. "This is temporary. Soon enough, you'll be with your future fancy husband."

The one whose enormous household she intended to manage whilst repressing her own interests and talents for the rest of her life.

"I hope so," Lady Felicity acknowledged after a moment. Her shoulders curved. "I recently suffered a minor setback, but I'm certain I'll turn things around."

Ah. So the future fancy husband was not a nebulous dream, but a flesh-and-blood man. Some stuffy, pretentious bore who required an equally stuffy, pretentious bore as his wife.

Giles could not help but be disappointed that the woman he'd known as Stable Lass would accept such a fate without a fight. He'd hoped she would show more spirit.

"Can't you find a rich toff with room in his mews for his mechanically inclined wife?"

She tossed him a pitying look.

"Of course *you* wouldn't understand," she said with a sigh. "Ladies are expected to be ladylike. There are infinitely more rules than you imagine. I shan't have a fancy future husband or be mistress of a household if I don't perfectly adhere to expectations."

Her tone rankled. Of course *he* wouldn't understand. He was nothing but an unimportant blacksmith, plying a lowly manual trade, eking out a dismal plebeian existence, save for the glorious moments in which his vaunted clientele condescended to speak with him, or allow him to service their carriage.

Giles knew what *he* would suggest she do with her hoity-toity rules and grandiose airs.

"That's what matters most?" he asked with feigned politeness. "Wealth and status at all costs?"

"At *any* cost," she agreed fervently. "God willing."

His lip curled. He'd thought she was different than the others. Maybe she even was. But she didn't want to be. Striving to be a replica of every other high-flown aristocrat was far worse than having been born unctuous and superficial. This was her *choice*. The sort of life she wanted to live.

He was glad their unwilling partnership had an end date. In fact, there was little reason for their paths to intertwine. They'd been working on these carriages in tandem for years without meeting. Given what he now knew about her, the best course was to return to being strangers.

"I will drop by every afternoon at this time to keep my eye on the curricle," he said as evenly as possible. "Feel free to leave your suggestions in written form, if you'd like to avoid meeting in person."

"Thank you for the idea," she said after the briefest pause.

There. The temporary "partnership" needn't affect either of their lives one whit.

CHAPTER 3

The next morning, dawn had barely broken when Felicity marched down the dark corridor leading from the town house to the carriage house. Attempting to forget the Curricle King's clear dismissal had only resulted in a sleepless night as their final words repeated again and again in her head.

She opened the latch and pushed open the door. A dust-speckled shaft of early morning light swept into the corridor along with a gust of cool, spring air. Usually, Felicity barreled eagerly over the threshold, straight to one of the carriages.

Today, she lingered in the doorway.

As much as she loved the opulence of the town house, the carriage house was where she had always felt most at home. It was supposed to be her private space, her secret haven, and it had been… until Cole invited a usurper. The unbearably arrogant, wildly attractive, *I-work-alone* Giles Langford.

Even though all outsiders were now forbidden from the carriage house, her pantalettes and worn dress no longer felt like a sufficient disguise. These clothes had never been comfortable. Now they didn't even feel safe.

More than ever, she wished for a man's shirt and thick trousers, and a woolen cap to shove her hair out of sight. She wished Cole hadn't forbidden male clothes. In a carriage house, she still felt more comfortable dressed as a lad than a lady. Her delicate kid half-boots felt glued to the stone, unable to step onto the sawdust.

"Good morning," said one of the stable boys as he passed. "Off to the races?"

The back of Felicity's neck heated. She stepped out of the corridor and shut the door behind her.

"No," she assured him quickly. "Today I'm going to work on—" She stopped, reconsidered his words, and narrowed her eyes. "What races?"

"The races," he said, gaze shining. "You usually don't start work until later in the morning, so I figure the reason you're down at dawn is to see who wins."

Races at dawn could only mean wealthy gentlemen wagering over the fastest horse or lightest chariot over in Hyde Park.

Felicity had never attended. Such attractions weren't open to respectable ladies, although the right clothes and the early hour would provide cover enough.

But she had better things to do. Like prove to Giles Langford she was every bit as competent as he was.

"Who do you think will win?" she asked the stable boy.

He gave her a strange look. "The Curricle King, of course. What I wouldn't give to watch him in action."

By the way that moniker was constantly bandied about in the carriage house, if Felicity's brother wasn't paying his stablehands handsomely, every one of them would be lining Rotten Row right now, hoping for a glimpse of Giles Langford.

And if the increased tempo of Felicity's heart was anything to go by, a tiny—very well, *large*—part of her found this to be an excellent idea. She gave in to temptation.

"Come along," she said as she grabbed an oversized pelisse and a straw bonnet from a basket in the corner. She always kept coins in her pocket in case of emergency.

The boy hurried after her. "Where are we going?"

"To hail a hack," Felicity answered as the limp brim of the ragged bonnet flopped down over her face. It was perfect.

"A hack?" The boy gestured over his shoulder. "You have seven different carriages."

"Colehaven owns those." Although Felicity regularly drove her brother's many carriages under cover of night, morning had broken, and she could not risk being recognized. She hurried down the alley toward the main street and held out her arm to flag a passing hackney. "Come on. You and I are just two ordinary citizens, off to the races."

His eyes lit up and he leaped into the hack behind her with a wide, gap-toothed smile on his freckled face.

If Felicity could have worn trousers, she wouldn't have needed a chaperone. To be honest, she probably didn't need one now, not in this unassuming garb—but she didn't have the heart to leave the starry-eyed boy behind.

"Rotten Row," she told the driver, and settled onto the squab.

"Are you excited to see the Curricle King?" the boy asked.

More than Felicity dared admit.

Langford was an enigma. Reading about his exploits in scandal columns could not possibly compare to witnessing his conquests firsthand. The baffling man had unconditionally accepted a female mechanic, only to imply in no uncertain terms that he had little use for *Lady Felicity* taking up his precious time or space once he realized just who the stable lass truly was.

"I'd trust him with any carriage," she answered at last. "But in order to design modifications to best complement a driver, I first need to see that driver in action."

This was her opportunity to observe him in his natural habitat… and find out if women really did dampen their bodices and swoon at the sight of him.

The boy frowned. "I heard him tell you, 'No modifications.'"

"He did say that," Felicity agreed. "I also heard His Grace clearly state that he wanted to *win*. Our loyalties must lie with him."

"He won't just win." A smug smile spread across the boy's face. "With you and the Curricle King as a team, the duke will *destroy* the competition."

As flattering as the boy's confidence was, Felicity and Langford were a team in only the weakest of definitions. She straightened her shoulders. With luck, today's field research would help her gain an advantage.

"Hyde Park," said the driver as he pulled the hack to a stop.

Felicity's pulse quickened as she alighted to a crowded street.

Hyde Park at dawn was the preferred ground for illegal duels or semi-legal races, and an endless stream of foot traffic swarmed toward Rotten Row as if the road were paved with gold sovereigns.

"I'm guessing we go this way," she told the

boy dryly as they melted into the flow of people.

Faster than she would have anticipated, they reached the edge of the track, a few dozen yards from where several smart curricles stood at the ready. Felicity moved to the front for a better view.

"This is madness," she murmured—or would have murmured, if it were possible for anything lower than a shout to be heard over the roar of voices. "It's as if these people expect the Prince Regent to roll by."

"Even better, dearie," a girl to her left said with a conspiratorial wink. "You're about to see *Giles Langford.*"

Felicity might have scoffed, had the sound of his name not sent a delicious shiver of anticipation tingling down her spine.

She was far from alone. Excitement was palpable. The brisk chill in the air had been replaced by the warmth of hundreds of bustling bodies, rubbing shoulders as they crowded to line the dirt-packed road. Even though she was disguised, Felicity was grateful she didn't glimpse any rich gentlemen she knew.

"Have you seen Langford race before?" she asked the girl.

"Every time I can," the girl replied without hesitation.

Several others nodded at this response, men and women alike.

"There he is!" squealed the girl.

Felicity jerked her gaze away from her fellow spectators and back toward the row of smart curricles, where groomsmen were handing off the reins to dashing, well-dressed drivers. How she wished she could race alongside them!

Langford's curricle was near the rear of the queue. All the drivers exchanged pleasantries with spectators as they inched toward the starting line. In moments, Giles Langford would pass directly in front of Felicity.

"That's his baby," said a man to her right.

Felicity leaned forward eagerly. "The legendary 'Baby?'"

"The custom curricle he built by hand," another man said in awe. "Won't let anyone but himself sit in the driver's seat."

Looking at this crowd, Felicity realized Langford did not *need* to race lordlings' carriages to be welcomed among them. In this arena, Langford was king and everyone else his mere subject.

"Too bad the race is only half an hour," said a woman.

"Some come for the races," another woman explained. "The rest of us could gaze at Langford all day."

Of that, Felicity had no doubt. She forced herself to focus her attention on the chaise, rather than the equally breathtaking man at the reins. Until today, she'd only seen "Baby" in penny caricatures. What was it about this particular design that gave him greater advantage? How could she incorporate similar elements into Cole's curricle in time for that race?

"Here they come!" another woman whispered, fanning her throat.

The crush of bodies pushed dangerously forward as the curricles rolled toward the starting line.

"How's Baby feeling today?" a man called out.

Felicity craned her neck to try and see Langford's reaction.

He grinned at the crowd and shouted back, "Stand back, for your safety. Baby's stronger than ever!"

Laughter and renewed excitement rippled through the crowd.

Felicity gazed about in awe and disbelief. Giles Langford was so famous that even his *chariot* was infamous.

She watched as he effortlessly charmed his admirers with relaxed banter and gracious style. He looked like a normal, friendly gentleman out for a casual ride, rather than a fearless whip about to decimate his competition in a high-energy race in front of hundreds of witnesses.

For a fervent moment, she didn't wish she was dressed like a lad, but as a grown man, so that she too could feel the bracing wind in her hair as she raced alongside the others. It wouldn't even matter if she lost, so long as she was part of the excitement and camaraderie and challenge. Her blood pulsed with excitement.

Now more than ever, she was determined to ensure her brother's carriage—and its driver—had every possible advantage.

When Langford's carriage passed right in front of her, she expected his attention to fall on one of the many noisy admirers flanking her.

Instead, he pulled his curricle to a halt and touched the brim of his hat.

"Lady Mechanic." His slow, devastating smile caused a wave of coos and sighs among the women on either side of her.

"Mr. King," she replied. Of course he would recognize her dressed in her dowdiest clothes. This was how she'd looked when they'd met. To him, a gown fit for a ball would seem like the disguise. Nonetheless, she was glad the floppy brim of her bonnet hid her face from the rest of the crowd.

He leaned forward, as if he had all the time in the world. "What lures you out of your carriage house?"

"You," she answered honestly, and immediately wished she had not. Heat was rising up the back of her neck.

His smile widened and his cobalt blue gaze stayed focused on her.

"Your baby," she heard herself babbling. "I mean your curricle. I'd never seen the one that you built yourself."

"You *do* appreciate the finer things," he teased. "If I'd known all it would take to impress you was to spend six months perfecting designs and toiling before the fire in order to—"

"Langford!" called one of the other drivers. "When that pistol goes off, we're racing with or without you!"

"We'll continue this later," he stage-whispered, and trotted off to join the others.

Felicity stared after him, openmouthed.

He'd wanted to impress her? The daft man had been impressing her since the first moment she read of his exploits. She'd confirmed his expertise with her brother, who well knew how to recognize talent. Langford was a legend.

His racing wins had impressed her, his smithing ability had impressed her, his nonchalance when faced with a female mechanic had impressed her. His ability to draw large crowds impressed her, his happy-go-lucky interactions with his admirers impressed her, his hand-built carriage—

A pistol shot blasted through the air.

In a cloud of dust, eight carriages shot off down the lane, two by two.

Langford was at the rear but wouldn't be for long. Already he was overtaking the seventh carriage, the sixth, the fifth. Turning around at the end of the straight dirt track would require even more precision.

"When he makes it back to the finish line, you won't even *see* the others," predicted a man to her right.

To her consternation, Felicity was no longer mentally cataloguing the size and width of the wheels or the length of the splinter bar and breeching dee, but staring after Giles Langford. The man looked like a god of chariots.

He had no prayer of blending with high society, nor any desire to try. He didn't need to. He was precisely who and what he appeared to be.

And the more he made no attempt to put on airs or conform to expectations… the more he simply accepted her, as though it was perfectly normal to chat about carriages on the side of the road with a lady coach smith, the harder he became to resist.

Thank heavens he'd dashed off at the crack of the pistol. Who knew what behavior Felicity might have been reduced to if he'd kept flirting with her despite her tattered clothes and the legions of adoring women jostling for a better view.

It took little over ten minutes for the first carriages to reach the far end of the track. During that time, Langford managed to weave his way from the back to the very front. For the second half of the race, she had an unob-structed view of him riding well in front; a king leading a parade to the admiration of his subjects.

He was magnificent.

Out of self-preservation, she took a deep breath and stepped back from the crowd to-ward the shade of a tree before he made it back to where she'd stood. His competency and obvious superiority was breathtakingly attractive. Her heart pounded unnaturally loud in her ears. She did not have time for a silly infatuation, she reminded herself.

Yet her heart leaped as she watched him race. As if the two of them *were* a team, and his conquest was her conquest, too.

Had she thought she was a skilled driver? Langford coasted between carriages with barely an inch to spare, his posture just as re-laxed as his horses, as if they made runs like this every day of the year. No one else stood a chance.

As Langford brought his horses back to the finish line—well ahead of his competition— his animated gaze hunted through the crowd where Felicity had just stood. His smile dimmed for scarcely a moment.

Perhaps most people would not have noticed.

Felicity noticed.

She feared her heart would never be the same.

CHAPTER 4

Felicity gazed up at her newest dance partner with a creeping sense of dread. Now that Lord Raymore was no longer an option, she needed to leave tonight's soirée with at least one potential suitor on the hook. Even if it meant this one.

Lord Kenwood was not her first choice in husbands for a variety of reasons. The earl didn't bother to sit in the House of Lords, only one of his properties was safely entailed, and he frequently made "jests" such as *the best women are buxom women*.

Felicity was not as curvaceous as some ladies, but with the right bodice and the right undergarments, she could catch a man's eye. Like tonight. Lord Kenwood had begged for a dance the moment her décolletage entered the ballroom.

"What a charming gown," the earl murmured.

He lowered his head, ostensibly to whisper into her ear, but when no further commentary was forthcoming, Felicity was forced to presume he'd simply angled for a better look down her bosom.

"Thank you." She answered with a smile despite the urge to scream.

Felicity had actually *liked* Lord Raymore. But her aversion to Lord Kenwood's greasy personality was not a factor. Marrying a well-situated husband was a woman's best chance to shape her future. And Felicity had much bigger plans than chasing her own comfort. She would do *anything* to help children who could not help themselves.

If that meant being wed to a man like Lord Kenwood for the rest of her life, then so be it. A countess could be quite powerful. That was, if an earl like this could be convinced to sign a betrothal contract allowing his wife to use a portion of their wealth for charitable works.

Lord Kenwood leaned a little too close. "Would you like to take a turn in the garden after this set?"

"It's raining," Felicity pointed out, then forced herself to add, "else I would have loved to."

The earl glanced over his shoulder at the rivulets of cold rain dripping down the open garden doors in surprise and dismay. He clearly had not been hoping to enjoy the weather, but rather an unobserved private moment with Felicity and her artfully arranged bosom. Her stomach turned.

She hated that she had to try so hard to attract a man like this.

"One day soon when the sun is out," Lord Kenwood said, "why don't we take an afternoon promenade through Hyde Park in my phaeton?"

This was it. The opening she'd been hoping for, the chance to be seen as something more than a mere dance partner. A potential courtship, on display before all and sundry.

Yet at the words Hyde Park, the only "sundry" on Felicity's mind was handsome, talented Giles Langford. Might he be there at the same time? What would he think to see her locked to the earl's side as they paraded by their peers in a high-flying phaeton?

For a foolish moment, she wished that it was Langford who had invited her to the park, that she were dancing in Langford's arms, rather than the earl's. Did Langford know how to waltz? Felicity shoved the thought aside. She didn't know and it didn't matter. Her job was to make a good match.

"A marvelous idea," she said aloud. "I love carriages."

Lord Kenwood gave her a kind but pitying look, as if he doubted that she could tell a barouche from a landau, but would condescend to escort her and her bosom all the same. She would have to be careful not to spoil the assumption.

When the music ended, the earl returned her to the group of friends she'd been chatting with before her set with Lord Kenwood, then escorted Lady Penelope Wakefield to the dance floor. When the music began, Felicity's teeth clenched. Perhaps she had misread the earl's intentions after all.

"A waltz," she groaned so low that only Hester Donnell might overhear.

"A hundred waltzes wouldn't deviate Lady Penelope from her path," Hester promised. "Lord Findon will whisk her to the altar before the Season is through."

Felicity wished she were half as certain as Hester. "Is Lord Raymore just as smitten?"

Hester pointed the edge of her fan across the ballroom, where the gray-haired marquess whirled the lovely Miss Corning in time to the music.

Felicity gasped. "Second waltz in one night?"

"Practically a public proposal," Hester agreed. "His offer is forthcoming, if he hasn't made it already."

"That was… fast," Felicity said faintly. She'd been trying to attract the earl since long before Miss Corning's debut.

Hester wrinkled her nose as if deciding whether or not to reveal a secret, then at last sighed and lowered her fan. "The gossips claim Raymore *would* have picked you, had you not been on the shelf for so long. You have good hair and pretty eyes, but the marquess likes a certain type. Your flaw is that you're old."

The advanced age of four-and-twenty was far from Felicity's only flaw. She'd had several suitors, none of whom came up to scratch at the final hour. The charitable works clause repelled every last one of them.

Worse, image was everything to aristocrats. If Lord Raymore's peers didn't want Felicity... the marquess didn't want her, either. Not when there were so many pretty debutantes floating about. She curled her hands into fists.

"It's an inescapable curse," she said to Hester. "If I haven't been snatched up by now, there must be something wrong with me. The mere fact that I'm available makes men run the other way."

Hester shivered. "I would die if that happened to me. If I didn't have Titus, I'd marry the first lord who asked."

Was that what Felicity should have done? Marry the first lord who asked, and simply *hope* he could be talked into philanthropy?

Hester wasn't heartless. She was one of several aristocrats who donated books and money to the Children's Circulating Library, a small but well-received initiative designed to improve the minds of London's youth. Subscriptions were still expensive enough that only families at a certain level could take part, but it was a step in the right direction and gave Felicity hope.

"If you weren't already betrothed, what would you look for in a husband?" she asked.

"A title," Hester replied without hesitation. "I want to have a husband in the House of Lords. What about you?"

Felicity had thought about this question endlessly. Security was the first concern. A homeless woman necessarily must concentrate on her wellbeing to the exclusion of others.

Money was the second-most important factor. She'd use it to create a Foundation for Impoverished Children and spend every possible moment helping those who had never been spoiled or coddled in their lives.

"If it were up to me," she said, "I would—"

Before she could finish her thought, a debutante in white ran by sobbing, and nearly plowed straight into a plaster column.

Felicity grabbed the girl's arm just before she would have crashed.

"Shh," she soothed. "Take a moment to breathe. Whatever it is—" Felicity blinked. "Miss *Corning?* I thought you were dancing with Lord Raymore!"

"I was," the girl said between sniffles.

Felicity's hackles rose in alarm. "If he manhandled you without your consent—"

"He wouldn't touch me with a ten-foot pole," Miss Corning sobbed. "I've lost his interest entirely."

Even Hester looked gobsmacked by this. "What on earth happened?"

"He asked me what I thought the best part about being a lady was, and I said, 'The money to spoil oneself, of course.'" Miss Corning lifted her chin defensively. "It's what Mama always told me."

Felicity winced. "What did he say to that?"

"He said 'what about children?' And I said, 'No expense will be spared when it comes to spoiling my children.' And he said, 'What about other people's children?' And I said, 'Obviously they're their own parents' responsibility. A lady cannot be expected to finance every child in the entire world, can she?'"

"Let me guess," Hester said dryly. "Raymore disagrees?"

"He doesn't just disagree." Miss Corning's lower lip trembled. "He's on a *child labor reform committee*, and hopes to do more. He said we're not suited at all!"

"Good God," Hester said with a straight face. "Not a *child labor reform committee*."

Felicity's head was spinning. She felt bad for Miss Corning, but clearly this wasn't her best match. The news filled Felicity with hope. Raymore was actively seeking new charitable works… and was back on the Marriage Mart?

"My life is over," Miss Corning wailed.

"Once everyone finds out Lord Raymore withdrew his suit, I'll *never* find a husband. I've fallen from 'diamond of the first water' to 'avoid like the plague' in the space of a waltz. I'm ruined."

She pushed away and ran off toward the retiring room before Felicity or Hester could reply.

"Miss Corning might be naïve and a bit self-centered, but she isn't *ruined*," Felicity offered after a moment of awkward silence. "Is she?"

"Worse," Hester intoned darkly. "She's right. Raymore's interest made her popular, but his disinterest makes her anathema. With no title in her family and no impressive dowry to offer, Miss Corning didn't just lose a suitor. She might have lost her chance."

Felicity did not ask how Hester knew the details of Miss Corning's dowry. Hester knew everything.

Well, almost everything. Hester did not know about Felicity's life before she and her brother came to London. And Hester did not know Felicity still loved to spend her free time tinkering with carriages. It was too dear a secret to tell.

To marry well, Felicity needed to keep her place in society. Which meant, after the upcoming curricle race... no more tinkering in the family mews.

In fact, visiting the ducal carriage house at

all was too much of a risk. The doors to the alley were open for light. Even with the increased guards, the wrong person might see in and deduce her identity.

If she was going to help her brother's carriage win the race, she'd have to do so under significantly more cover. She needed someplace where the pinks of the ton would send a servant as their emissary, or at the very least, never expect to come across the sister of a duke.

Somewhere like Giles Langford's private smithy.

CHAPTER 5

*G*iles crossed his arms in satisfaction as he watched the bustling activity in his busy smithy.

This was happiness. Work he was good at, a shop he was proud of, and someone to share it with. Plenty of someones. Giles was used to waking every morning content with his life. He never longed for things he didn't possess. Enjoying what he was fortunate enough to have was more than enough cause for joy.

"I saw you at the races," one of the boys said shyly.

Giles raised a brow. "Did you?"

"We all did," said another, eyes shining. "What does it feel like to be faster than everyone else?"

Giles didn't bother with false modesty. He was paid well for a reason: his patrons expected to *win*. Being able to race his own carriage once in a while was a delight he would never tire of.

"It's magical," he said slowly, as he tried to put the feeling into words. "The air rushes in your ears as though you've just leaped from a tall tree into a lake, but you're not falling. You're *flying*. Your cheeks are ruddy and cold, and you must squint in order to see against the sun and the wind, but despite the clatter of wheels and the thunder of hooves, it feels like *you* are the one soaring straight and true, an unstoppable arrow that no one can catch."

"That's exactly what it looks like," breathed one of the lads in awe.

"It's the most exciting thing I've ever seen," said another.

"Mind your posts," Giles reminded them. "Breaks are for talking."

They hurried back to their stations.

Giles leaned his shoulders against a wall. He was not surprised to hear the lads ask about the races. It was a frequent topic here in his workshop, particularly any day following the release of a caricature portraying him flying down a track so fast that only the tips of his competitors' hats were visible above clouds of dust. His lips quirked.

What would the scandalmongers think to see their reckless, fearless rebel serving biscuits and lemonade to a bunch of neighborhood children?

His name would appear in White's betting

book the next evening, Giles realized wryly, along with high-profile wagers as to how many weeks or months remained before Giles set about fathering children of his own... or whether he *had* fathered all these boys.

The jest would be on them.

Giles had no intention of starting a family any time soon. Or taking a wife. It would necessarily take time away from his work, as well as from his time with lads like these who had come to rely on him. Many had little at home and even fewer prospects. The opportunity to learn a trade gave them hope when before they had none.

Besides, he loved his life just as it was. Comfortable and fun, thrilling and industrious. The last thing he needed was a wrench thrown into the mix.

"This is your idea of 'I work alone?'" came a droll female voice just outside his smithy.

Lady Felicity.

His walking, talking wrench.

He jerked his spine up straight. "These are my helpers. I am their master. Are you here to be my apprentice?"

Her eyes danced as a tiny smirk twitched at the edges of her plump lips.

"I am here as a carriage counselor." She gestured behind her, where the Duke of Colehaven's horses were tied to a post. "Is there room in the inn for another curricle?"

Giles crossed his arms. "What makes you think I—"

"Station five is empty," said one of his apprentices.

"We could also ready station two in a trice," added another.

"Fine." Giles made shooing motions to his acolytes. "Station five. Go."

After this, he was going to have to have a stern conversation with the Duke of Colehaven. If His Grace disliked invited guests dropping by ahead of schedule, how did he think Giles might react to the unexpected delivery of a carriage?

"Tell your brother there's a storage fee," he informed Lady Felicity as the curricle was eased into its new home.

She narrowed her eyes. "You're just hoping to be rid of me."

He inclined his head. "The curricle has arrived safely. Aren't you going?"

"I'm your new carriage counselor," she repeated with the arch of a brow. "Where this curricle goes, I go. And it's staying here until you win the race."

"You cannot possibly expect to move in with it."

"Why not?" She widened her eyes innocently. "You don't live inside the actual forge, do you?"

"He lives upstairs," said one of the lads.

"With his mother," added another.

"Future apprentices," Giles enunciated distinctly, "should be seen and not heard."

One of the lads frowned. "I thought that was 'children.'"

"Or 'ladies,'" suggested another.

"We can all hear *her*," pointed out a third.

Lady Felicity eased into the shop and reached out a finger to touch his workbench.

Giles stepped closer. "No hands-on unless I specifically say so, Miss Carriage Counselor."

She paused with her finger above a swage block and cocked an eyebrow in his direction. "None at all?"

He smiled politely. "My smithy, my rules."

She lowered her hand and smiled back. "And what are the rules, Curricle King?"

"Lemonade before aprons," said one of the lads.

"Don't stoke the fire without gloves," said another.

"Say 'thank you' if someone gives you a biscuit," said a third.

"*Hard* taskmaster," Lady Felicity mouthed in his direction as she made her way toward the decimated refreshment table. "There appears to be neither lemonade nor biscuits."

"That's because you cocked up rule number one," one of the lads said. "Arrive first, if you're hungry."

"You can't say 'cock up' in front of a lady," whispered another in horror.

"I don't mind," Lady Felicity assured them. "He can say 'cock up' all he likes."

All six lads gasped like pious grandmothers.

"To your stations," Giles ordered. He grasped Lady Felicity's elbow and led her out of eyesight behind a viscount's barouche. "Does your brother know you're here?"

"I came with his blessing," she answered. "After you infiltrated our carriage house—"

His jaw fell open. "I scarcely infiltrated—"

"—I no longer feel safe working there," she finished. A shadow fell over her eyes, but she blinked it away.

He stared at her in disbelief. "You don't feel safe in your own home, but you feel safe in mine?"

"Safe from discovery," she clarified, and gestured toward her torso. "Hence the disguise."

It took him a moment to realize that she was garbed much as she'd been dressed the morning that he'd seen her at the races—and that a droopy bonnet, tattered pelisse, and stained gown was not precisely the elegant attire one more commonly associated with the sister of a duke.

"Of course," he said. "I wondered about the disguise."

She fluttered her eyes heavenward and let out a world-weary sigh. "You didn't even *notice* the disguise."

"To be fair," he pointed out, "the disguise was the least surprising component of the unexpected arrival of a ducal curricle and self-appointed 'carriage counselor.'"

"Duke-appointed," she assured him. "You were standing right there when Cole insisted we work together. And this arrangement is perfect. No one would look for me here, and with so many others milling about… nobody will notice one more worker."

Giles would notice. He would spend every moment of every day noticing every curve and sigh and lick of the lips. And there was nothing he could do about it until after the race.

He gestured behind him in defeat. "Aprons in the pile to the left, gloves in the bucket to the right."

She blinked. "That's it?"

"That's what?"

"No argument?" she stammered, as if he was the one throwing wrenches. "I show up unannounced, and you're not patting me on the head and shooing me from your very manly workshop?"

"First of all," he said, "No one wants to touch that bonnet."

She inclined her head. "True."

"Secondly," he continued, "you're right. I *was* standing right there when Colehaven commanded us to work together. More importantly, you've spent more time with this curricle than anyone, and you know what you're about. Go get an apron."

Cheeks flushing a becoming pink, Lady Felicity laid her bonnet on the table as she pulled an apron over her head.

"Hats on the hooks," someone called out.

"Right." She crossed the room to place her bonnet on an empty nail next to the row of boys' caps, then turned back toward Giles. "You *do* have a lot of rules."

"He's the master," one of the lads said simply. "That's one of the most important rules of all."

Lady Felicity shot Giles an arch look.

He smiled back at her blandly.

"You'll never be *my* master," she warned him. "You may be the master of your shop, but I am the master of my brother's carriage."

He tossed her a large rag. "Rule number thirty-seven: Carriage-master keeps his assigned carriage clean of dirt and grime."

"I doubt that's a real rule," she muttered as she began wiping the dust from the curricle's exterior.

Giles grinned as he pulled a rag from his apron and joined her.

The next quarter hour passed with companionable ribbing and semi-serious debates about the virtues of leather washer seals and the various styles of axle grease. Every shared laugh caused a strange flutter in his stomach.

Bickering with Lady Felicity as they

worked together on a carriage was *almost* as much fun as preparing his own curricle for a race. It would be a challenge to keep her away from—

She followed his line of sight and visibly restrained herself from bouncing on her toes. "That's 'Baby,' isn't it? She's gorgeous. May I see her up close?"

"You may not."

"I just want to—"

"Nobody touches Baby," he said firmly. "In fact, the only carriage you have permission to touch belongs to your brother."

"But she's been custom-built specifically to your taste," Lady Felicity protested. "You know how much I love personalized modifications."

"I don't recall the subject ever coming up."

"Well, now you know." She inched in the direction of his curricle. "If you would just let me—"

"No," he said before she could continue. "Baby is my business. Your brother is yours."

"Arrogant and overbearing," she muttered with narrowed eyes. "And to think, this is what I have to look forward to when I marry."

"You're not marrying *me*," he pointed out in alarm.

"Of course not," she said with a laugh. "But I don't imagine earls and dukes to be less imperious."

That it was true did not make it any less irritating.

"Which are you settling for?" he enquired in a bored voice. "A duke or an earl?"

"I'm down to one name on the list," she replied sweetly, "and it isn't yours."

"You have a *list?*" He could just imagine a parchment full of Lord This, Lord That, all with a line through their names. It was even more insulting than he'd guessed. Apparently even rich, handsome lordlings could fail to meet Lady Felicity's exalted criteria.

Someone like Giles would never even be considered.

He shouldn't care. And yet, to his shock, he *did*.

"Who's the lucky gentleman?" He busied himself with the front axle to hide his irritation. "Sedgwick?"

"No. A spendthrift," she answered.

"Lord Findon?"

"All but betrothed to Lady Penelope." At his blank expression, she added, "Wakefield. She's a marquess's daughter."

Giles sifted his memory for the names of the titled gentlemen that visited his favorite tavern, the Wicked Duke. Most of them were Giles's customers. One in particular could be considered the smithy's biggest account. "Not... Lord Raymore?"

Her eyes widened in surprise. "You know him?"

One could say that.

Raymore was always dropping off this carriage or that. He'd been a valued client for years. Giles clenched his jaw. He would have to congratulate the happy couple on their nuptials as if these moments with Lady Felicity had never happened. Giles would stand right here for the next decade or two, watching Lord and *Lady* Raymore ride off together again and again.

It shouldn't bother him. But it did.

"What's so wonderful about Raymore?" he grumbled. He could guess the answer.

"Wealthy, titled, in possession of multiple entailed properties, sits in the House of Lords, *and*—" She paused for effect. "—newly back on the market."

He tightened a wheel bolt. Being right was not always fun. Lady Felicity was an unapologetic fortune-hunter and social climber. Instead of possessing a mere courtesy title, she'd soon be a peer. Married to a rich marquess with "multiple entailed properties." No mention of whether she actually *liked* the man.

"You think Lord Raymore will allow his wife to work on carriages?"

"Absolutely not," she replied, her brown eyes serious. "In fact, he'll never know it ever happened. Once you win Cole's race, I shan't work on carriages ever again."

Giles frowned. "Even if you're not married yet?"

"Even if I'm not married yet," she agreed. But the happiness had left her face. "He hasn't exactly asked. So far all we've shared are waltzes, but—"

"You're preemptively subjugating your desires to an unfamiliar man who hasn't offered for you yet," Giles said in disbelief. "That's—"

"*Strategy*," Lady Felicity finished. "He'll ask if I can make him believe I'm what he wants."

No. Giles curled his lip. She meant the marquess would marry her if she could *become* what he wanted. That was what was so disappointing. Lady Felicity had seemed like so much *more*.

Or perhaps he, too, wanted her to be something she was not.

"I cannot abide stuffy, pretentious people," Giles said.

"How awkward. I aspire to be a stuffy, pretentious lady," she informed him, "married to a stuffy, pretentious lord with a stuffy, pretentious estate. What do you care?"

"It makes you sound selfish," he muttered.

"And I am," she agreed. "We all are, to some degree. Not that it's any of your business what my husband and I do with our lives, but I intend to fund a charity."

Giles paused with one hand on the splinter bar. "A what?"

"A charitable foundation to aid children in need. Food, housing, education. I hope to make it a large affair, with so many helpers we'll never have to turn away a single child."

It sounded… admirable. Some of his disdain fell away.

"Will your future husband allow you to volunteer in such a place?"

"The marquess would allow me to donate funds," she hedged.

Not quite the same thing, but even Giles could see why Raymore was the one man who made her list. His wealth, his power, his position…

"He's passionate about charitable works," Lady Felicity added. "He even leads a committee."

Huzzah for Lord Raymore.

"You could volunteer *here*," Giles heard himself say. "If you wanted to do more. There are always more neighborhood lads than my journeymen and I have time to mentor."

"If *you* wanted to do more," she replied archly, "you could welcome a few lasses. Lads aren't the only creatures capable of tightening a wheel nut. Or is your charity only open to boys?"

"It's not a charity," he protested. "It's a smithy."

A smithy in which the only artisan who had ever come close to being his father's equal had walked in the door wearing a frilly bonnet and day gown.

"A smithy for men," she said with a shrug.

"I thought you, perhaps, would not be so prejudiced."

Giles snapped his jaw closed. He hadn't welcomed a passel of local lads out of an explicit intent to exclude girls. Opening the smithy to their female counterparts hadn't crossed his mind at all.

Somehow, that almost made it worse.

"I don't just want to keep Cole's curricle in working condition," Lady Felicity continued, as if their discussion of eligible gentlemen and proper apprentices had never happened. "I want to improve it. The custom modifications would be based on my years of experience handling Cole's horses and your unique characteristics as the driver."

"You're asking for unconditional faith that everything will work out perfectly within the allotted time," he said flatly. "You want me to put the race in your hands."

"I want to take every advantage we have and maximize them." She licked her delectable lips. "I want to *win*. What do *you* want?"

To kiss you, came a little whisper from somewhere deep inside. *To show you that pots of gold and blue-blood titles aren't the only characteristics you should look for in a man.*

"Fine," he said.

Her eyes widened. "F-fine?"

"Call me arrogant and overbearing if you like, but I'm the best at what I do." He crossed his arms to keep from doing something foolish, like reaching for her. "So are you."

Her mouth fell open. "So am I?"

"Your brother says so. And this is his wager." Giles let out a slow breath. "You're just as motivated as I am to see me end the race in one piece and for Colehaven to win. Come back tomorrow at three. I'll clear the rest of my afternoon."

"Three o'clock it is," she said quickly, pulling off her leather apron with shaking fingers. She glanced over at him from beneath her lashes. "Tea time. I don't suppose we can heat a pot in the forge?"

"It's always best not to suppose," Giles agreed.

He placed her bonnet atop her head. The infernal floppy brim would keep his mouth well away from hers.

For now.

CHAPTER 6

*M*ost *important rule*, the lads had told her. *Arrive early.*

Felicity alighted from a hackney cab in front of Giles Langford's smithy at a quarter to three the following afternoon. Today, they would be equals. Two colleagues; the best at what they did.

Her skin tingled with excitement. She was just as eager for this as she had been for her debut in high society. The only way today could be better was if she could have burst inside wearing breeches and a work shirt instead of a patched-up day dress with hidden pantalettes.

She straightened her shoulders and marched in through the open doors. He wouldn't regret their partnership. She would prove to him she was worthy. He—

The smithy was empty.

Felicity frowned as she turned in a slow,

disbelieving circle. No master coach smith. No children.

Perhaps Langford had been called away unexpectedly and shut down the shop. She tried to mask her disappointment at the idea. Should she stay, in case he returned soon? Should she go, and await a new invitation?

Would there be another invitation if she left?

Felicity wasn't certain why working with Langford felt so important to her. As though their partnership might cease being one of her brother's many edicts, and could actually become… real.

At first, she thought these feelings were because Langford's shop reminded her so much of the old smithy where she and Cole had worked as children. But the two places couldn't be more different.

Langford's place was wide, airy, clean, well-stocked, *safe*. The children came of their own free will. They had gloves and aprons to wear. Refreshments to eat and drink.

Environments like this were exactly what her future foundation and committees like Lord Raymore's were fighting *for*. Children were not slaves or indentured servants, disposable tools to be worked until they fell apart and then discarded. They were people, and deserved to be treated like it.

The first year that she and her brother had lived in the grand town house on Grosvenor

Square, Cole had wanted them both to put the past behind them. His sister was a lady now. She had to learn to dress like one, act like one, talk like one. Cole wanted to give Felicity every possible opportunity that their new position afforded. Even though it meant denying who they used to be.

When she made her debut in society, Felicity was wise enough not to mention her past, but neither could she forget it. She didn't wish to. Those years had made her who she was. Forged her, cold and hard as iron, strong and unbreakable come what may.

When Cole had left one month to inspect the duchy's country estate, she had traveled back to the old smithy in secret, carrying a heavy purse on her lap. Her childhood friends would be shocked to discover Little Felix was now Lady Felicity, but she hoped a handful of coins for each one would buy a little forgiveness for abandoning them.

Except they weren't there. While she was off in London taking dancing lessons and shopping for ball gowns, they were at the forge day and night, working themselves sick. One was buried in an unmarked grave. Several had returned to the streets or worse. And the rest... Felicity would never know what had happened to them. The smithy was full of new children with gaunt faces and no more dreams.

She had sworn in that moment that she

would do everything in her power to save them. To save all of them. Every child in every workhouse, every chimneysweep, every barefoot angel with big eyes and an empty belly and no one to fight for them. *Felicity* would fight.

After returning home, she and Cole arranged a more reputable master for the old smithy, but it was one of a thousand. There was endless work to do. Cole dedicated every spare moment and penny, but he was one person. If Felicity married the right man, she could do more than double the donations. Once she'd convinced a powerful, titled husband to support the cause, his peers would follow suit.

With Lord Raymore's position and influence to back her, Felicity could convince the ton that children were worth fighting for. Or at least talk them into opening their pocketbooks. Raymore could use his position in the House of Lords to effect change at a national level, and Felicity's charitable foundation would change lives at a personal level.

If realizing this dream meant she had to give up her love of working on carriages to accomplish this, so be it. If honoring her vow meant she had to give up love altogether, so be it. Children's lives were worth the sacrifice.

In the meantime, she would enjoy every minute of freedom while she still had it. There was no telling when—

The rear door swung open and she whirled to face it.

Giles Langford stepped out into the smithy carrying a wooden tea tray, as if it were the most normal thing in the world to be doing so.

"Three o'clock is tea time," he reminded her as he placed the tray on the small table where the lads' repast had stood the day before. "Milk and sugar?"

"Thank you," she said faintly.

"Hats on hooks," he said as he lifted the pot and expertly began pouring the tea.

She yanked the ribbon loose from her chin and placed her bonnet on the nail she was already coming to think of as hers. It wasn't. She knew it wasn't. Yet part of her wished every tea time could be right here in this smithy.

As she accepted a cup of fresh, steaming tea, Felicity couldn't help but admit that the only predictable thing about Giles Langford was that he was impossible to predict.

"No lemon tarts?" she asked over the rim of her teacup.

The corner of his mouth twitched. "This is a smithy, not a bakery."

It also wasn't a tea garden, but the man made an impressive cup of tea.

"Where is everyone?" In her experience, most smithies stayed open from dawn to dusk.

"I gave everyone a few hours' free time so we could work on your brother's curricle without distractions." He clinked the edge of his cup against hers as if toasting with champagne. "To winning?"

She raised her cup in answer, unable to hide her grin. "To winning."

The wicked promise in his slow smile warmed her to her toes.

When she finished her tea, she placed the cup back on the tray and reached toward the pile of aprons.

"Going to crawl around the ground in a gown again?" he asked.

She slid him a vexed look. "Have you a better suggestion?"

"You tell me." He gestured to a small pile of clothing stacked on a three-legged wooden stool. "Want to borrow some trousers?"

She stared at him for a long moment, trying to work out his intent. Was this a jest, a farcical situation set up for him to be able to laugh at her? Or had the impossible man somehow seen straight into her soul?

His blank expression gave no clue.

"Y-yes," she said hesitantly. She would very much like to borrow some trousers.

He motioned to a folding screen in the corner of the shop, likely guarding a chamber pot. "I'll wait for you by the curricle."

With that, he lifted the tea tray and disappeared back through the rear door.

Felicity made her way toward the borrowed clothes and lifted them to her nose. Freshly laundered. Smartly folded. This had been done with just as much care to detail as the tea tray had been. The items even looked like they might fit.

Delighted, she hurried behind the folding screen, hoping to be out of her dress and into the clothes long before Langford returned.

Most days, fancy gowns felt like Felicity's battle armor. Patched trousers and a smudge of oil on her sleeve made her feel like there was no war to fight. Like she was precisely where and how she was supposed to be.

These trousers were a bit wide in the waist and snug in the hips. The white linen shirt was far too loose and the brown jersey tunic a little too long.

She hadn't worn clothes this comfortable in years.

A creak and the sound of a door latching back in place indicated Langford had returned to the smithy.

Suddenly shy and nervous, she forced herself to step out from behind the folding screen.

Langford did not rake a disdainful gaze up and down her mannishly clad frame or smirk at a subpar attempt to blend in. He simply raised his brows with polite interest.

"Better?"

"I feel like myself again," she confessed.

A satisfied smile reached the corners of his eyes.

"Giles Langford." He held out his hand. "Giles to my friends."

She placed her hand in his and gave a firm shake. "Lord… Felicity."

He burst out laughing. "Little Lord Felicity, is it? I'll remember that."

"I actually do answer to 'Felix,'" she confessed. And to *he*. And *him*. Masquerading as a little brother had been the key to her survival. Learning how to be a lady had begun with learning how to be female again. And learning what to do with stays… like the ones she'd left discarded behind the folding screen. The back of her neck heated. "But plain Felicity will do."

"You've never been plain a day in your life." His blue eyes held hers before he turned back toward the curricle. "What do you think about widening the wheels to be sturdier over rugged terrain?"

Felicity was not thinking about wheels at all. Had Giles Langford just implied he found her pretty?

"No comment?" He poked his head over the tail-board in surprise. "Somehow I assumed Lord Felix would be even more opinionated than Lady Felicity."

"No need for 'lord' or 'lady.' Partners should be on a first-name basis." She tilted her head at the carriage. "Wide wheels are heavy wheels. What do you think about narrower and lighter?"

And with that, they were off and running, any awkwardness forgotten. They perused every inch of the curricle, arguing and agreeing, guessing and teasing.

It wasn't until they were shoulder-to-shoulder beneath the chaise that Felicity realized how much easier it was to pass the time with Giles than to decipher ballroom mating dances.

Here with Giles, she was truly herself. Not just a woman in trousers, but a fellow coach smith in her own right. It was a heady, heart-pounding feeling.

Giles didn't speak to her as though he did so as a favor to her brother, or even in the same manner the lords she danced with spoke to debutantes. He treated her like she was his equal. As though there was nowhere this skilled, handsome man wished to be but right here at her side.

Felicity didn't notice she was staring until she realized he was gazing right back at her. Breath tangled in her lungs, but she couldn't look away. No matter how warm her cheeks had flushed.

She bit her lip to keep from blurting how she felt.

He tilted his head. "Colehaven says the only reason he entrusted his carriage to me instead of you is because I have a proper smithy and you don't."

She grinned. Not having a proper forge was the only valid excuse for one's brother to choose some other blacksmith over his own sister.

"Now you know what to get me for Christmas."

He affected an arrogant expression. "You'll never find a better smithy than mine."

True.

Neither said what they were both thinking. That this—whatever *this* was—would be over soon. There would be no Christmas. They could have nothing at all.

Except the continued pleasure of each other's company for the next eight days.

"I like your smithy," she said shyly. *And I like you.*

He glanced over at her in flattered surprise. "Do you?"

"Did you think I wouldn't?"

With a lift of his shoulder, he flashed a crooked smile. "It's a smithy."

"A splendid one." She cast her gaze about the palatial interior. "Clean, orderly, well-stocked, impressive…"

Being in his smithy was like visiting a toy shop. Every shelf and hook were full of new wonders, just waiting for her to explore. The workshop had an earthy, distinctive scent, a comfortable, inviting atmosphere, a feeling like… home.

Her chest thumped in alarm. This was not her cozy shop. She couldn't keep it *or* Giles. Her pulse fluttered at the idea. Appalled at the direction of her thoughts, she floundered for a way to ruin the moment.

"I'm sorry you disapprove of my husband-selecting process."

The jarring words shattered the companionable calm like a sledgehammer to ice. She could practically feel the cold shards raining down upon them.

"Most lords in town are my customers or friends from the Wicked Duke," Giles replied evenly. "I just hadn't expected to come across their names on a shopping list."

Felicity's face flushed with heat. There. She'd deserved that dig. Nor could she argue. Cole had created the initial list of approved prospects. Felicity had refined it. To Giles, she supposed "practical reasons" only made her seem more mercenary.

"I didn't know they were friends of yours," she muttered.

"Of course you didn't." A muscle worked at his temple. "A blacksmith, friends with Quality? Horrors." His lip curled and he looked away. "I despise when someone like you makes assumptions about everyone else."

Her eyebrows raised. "Someone like me?"

"Someone who thinks they're better than me."

Felicity's jaw dropped. "I don't think I'm better than you!"

"Why wouldn't you?" He counted on his fingers. "You have a fancy title and I don't. You live in a fancy neighborhood and I don't. You have fancy clothes and fancy airs and go to fancy parties and I don't. You have more connections, more money, more influence... Shall I go on? You probably even think you're the better coachmaker and driver."

"Just coachmaker," she snapped. "I'm the second-best driver."

He cast her a flat look.

"You're right," she said with a frustrated sigh. "Not that I think I'm better than you, but that in many ways, society thinks I am."

"*High* society," he corrected.

"High society," she agreed. "Point taken. Neither of us should make assumptions. Do you know why I started tinkering with carriages at a young age?"

"I do not," Giles answered.

Felicity bit her lip. Was she truly ready to share this part of her past? Would she *ever* be ready for someone to know all of her secrets?

"Indulgent parents?" Giles guessed.

"No," she said softly. "Suffice it to say, I know exactly how fortunate I am, and that I'm not any better than anyone else. If I was, one of the gentlemen on the list would have married me by now."

Practical reasons or not, she couldn't pretend it didn't sting. If any of her short-lived suitors had wanted Felicity as a person and not just as a bauble for their arms, they would have signed any betrothal clause her brother wished. That they preferred to select someone else to wed… well. Felicity couldn't let herself be hurt. She hadn't chosen them for their personalities either.

Marriage was a contract. A business decision. She could not allow feelings to get in the way.

"Is that really what you want?" Giles asked softly.

Felicity dropped her gaze. He was too big, too talented, too much. She loved every moment of working with him. Even dreamed about it at night. Of a world in which their partnership didn't have to be temporary. She curled her fingers about a head iron to withstand a rush of longing. Someday soon, she would have to walk away from Giles and his smithy and never look back. No matter how much doing so might hurt.

Ever since they'd met, a great yawning emptiness now filled her chest at the thought of everything she'd have to give up in order to fulfill her dream of giving more to those who needed it most.

If she broke the promise she'd made to the

children, she wouldn't simply be no better than anyone else.

She'd be worse.

Giles was perhaps the one person who would understand why she'd marry a wealthy man she despised over a penniless man she loved. There could be no higher goal than providing for children. She had not known they shared that in common, too, until yesterday. It only made her like him more.

He was a good man, but he was right about the differences in their social statuses. The charitable work in his smithy was the perfect example of what she hoped to see, but it would not change laws in the House of Lords. Felicity didn't want to help just one neighborhood. She'd vowed to help them all.

"Tell me about your local helpers," she said. "When did the lads start coming by?"

"The moment they smelled biscuits," Giles replied. "You might think rats have a keen sense of smell, but rodents are amateurs compared to twelve-year-old boys."

"Come for the lemonade, stay for slowly smelting iron over a blistering hot fire?" she asked dryly.

He flashed an irreverent smile. "Everyone has their price."

"What's yours?" she asked. "Do you get something from volunteering your time?"

"Children in the smithy," he answered without hesitation. "I loved my childhood. I spent every waking minute of it right here with my father."

She glanced around with interest. "This was your father's smithy?"

"A third of it used to be. I've since expanded twice. There's plenty of room for children to learn and grow. Someday, my offspring will also be following at my heels asking thousands of questions. But until I wed, the local children are more than enough."

Felicity felt as though a ball of ice had slammed into her midsection.

For years, she'd been consumed by the thought of when and whom she would marry. Never had it occurred to her that Giles—coach smith extraordinaire and fêted Curricle King—might share those same thoughts. Have his own nonnegotiable set of requirements. A list of bridal contenders in his pocket.

Her name would not be on it.

Giles's future wife was someone who would live with him here above the smithy, who would bring a wooden tray of lemonade down to the workshop, where her sons and daughters did their best to imitate their handsome father.

She shouldn't care what Giles did, Felicity reminded herself. She wasn't here for a romantic interlude, but to work on her brother's curricle. It didn't matter how free and relaxed she felt with him; how much at ease he put her with his pots of tea and borrowed trousers and complete confidence in her ability to dismantle and rebuild an even better carriage. How she wished he would kiss her.

Oh, who was she fooling? It took everything in her power not to launch herself into his arms right now.

The more he didn't try to make her fall in love with him, the more he simply accepted without question whatever she did or did not wish to do or give or share, the more she couldn't help but carve a secret place for him deep in the recesses of her heart.

Her hands shook. She had to get out of the smithy before she let her feelings get in the way of logic.

Felicity shot to her feet. "I—"

His hand touched her arm. "What is it?"

She forgot what it was. His hand was on her arm. Warm and strong through the thin sleeve.

Oh, blast. Not *her* sleeve. *His* sleeve. She was still wearing the clothes he'd arranged for her.

"I… ought to return your clothes," she managed.

His hand was still on her arm.

She hoped he never moved it.

"If you leave them here," he said, "they'll always be waiting for you on that stool, in exactly the same condition you found them today."

Was it possible to swoon over a gift of

boys' trousers? Yes. Yes, apparently it was indeed possible. Her heart would not stop racing.

"I'm sorry you always see me like… *this.*" She gestured at herself. Or meant to gesture at herself.

Apparently, her hand had an agenda of its own, because her fingertips now lightly grazed his arm. This wasn't *quite* an embrace —her fingers touching his upper arm, his thumb caressing just above her wrist—but they should definitely put a stop to it.

Right away.

Or perhaps in a few more minutes.

"I don't find you less beautiful because you aren't wearing some gown you hate," he said softly. "To me, you look the most beautiful any time you allow yourself to just be yourself, rather than pretend to be someone else."

"That's…" Words failed her.

He winced. "Too forward?"

Not forward enough.

She placed her trembling palms on either side of his muscular chest and met his cobalt blue gaze. "Since we met, I haven't stopped wondering what it would be like to kiss you."

"You cannot imagine how much I would love to help with that." He cradled her face in his rough hands as if she were the most precious thing he had ever touched. "But your brother—"

"—isn't here," she whispered. "No one is.

Just you and me. What are you going to do about it?"

He slanted his mouth over hers before she finished talking.

Had she thought a forge was hot? Those flames were nothing compared to the heat his kiss stoked deep within her. She slid her hands up his chest to his wide shoulders and laced her fingers behind his neck.

Now she was on her toes. A precarious position under normal circumstances, but circumstances were anything but normal. She was off-balance—had been off-balance from the moment she'd met him—but she need not worry about falling. He was here to catch her.

Her bosom pressed against his chest in the most deliciously wanton way. And her legs... dear heaven, her legs! Without a gown and shift to fill the space between them with cumbersome yards of fabric, she was free to press her legs against his, to feel the strength and heat of his thighs firm against her trembling limbs. In fact, she realized with growing arousal, she could even feel—

"Langford?" a male voice shouted from the street. "Are you in there?"

Felicity and Giles jumped apart panting, staring at each other with wide eyes still full of longing. If the seat rail of her brother's curricle hadn't blocked their kiss from view...

"Back here," Giles rasped as he straightened his clothing.

She tried to calm her heart. If Giles's voice shook after that kiss, God only knew what sort of croak might exit Felicity's throat if she foolishly tried to speak. She ran a hand down her bosom to try to smooth any wrinkles, then peeked around the carriage at the new visitor.

Visitors, plural.

The six lads from the day before, plus a tall man with auburn hair and a ready smile, and… two little girls?

The stranger bowed to Giles. "Kenneth's elder sister Maria and Norman's younger sister Beatrice, just as you requested."

Two of the lads beamed with brotherly pride.

With an equally wide smile, Giles motioned for Felicity to step out from her hiding place. "Allow me to present Hugh Tarleton, a rector of St. Giles. The lads, you met yesterday. Two are from Hugh's parish, and these are their sisters. Ladies, it is lovely to meet you."

The girls tittered.

Mr. Tarleton cleared his throat. "And who is…"

Felicity's heart skipped. Should she have stayed hidden? She didn't recognize this man, but—

"My mechanic," Giles replied easily.

His mechanic. Felicity wished she hated the sound of that. Instead, it sounded like music. Like belonging.

Mr. Tarleton bowed again, despite not being given her name.

"You're with the best," he assured her.

"*He's* with the best," she shot back with a grin.

The girls stared up at her with wide eyes. "Are you truly a lady mechanic?"

"One of the best, man or woman." Giles knelt to their height. "She's a master artisan. That means she's been an expert ever since she was your age."

Every child's eyes grew wide with wonder and awe.

Felicity wondered if Giles realized what a difference he'd made in their lives with one offhand comment. Not just for the girls, but for all the children. If Felicity could do it, they could do it too. There was a way out. They were all in the right place.

"Then they're all in good hands." Mr. Tarleton tipped his hat and left.

"Can I be *your* apprentice?" the youngest girl whispered to Felicity.

She longed to say yes. Like Giles, she yearned to someday teach her own children to tinker with tools and carriages. For them, it could be *fun* instead of solely a means for survival.

The fact that Giles had paid attention to her words... Not only listened to her perspective, but took immediate action to include female apprentices the very next day… Felicity's heart flipped. Had she thought the tea proved what sort of man he was? Had she believed a loaned set of trousers the greatest gift a non-family member had ever given her?

The inclusion of Beatrice and Maria was worth more than all the flowers in the world.

"I take it back," Felicity whispered to the girls. "I'm not the best. Mr. Langford is the best."

She would take advantage of every stolen moment she could have.

CHAPTER 7

Giles stood alone outside the doors of his smithy with a wicker basket by his feet.

After days of harmonious smithing—and several stolen kisses—he was tired of pretending the undeniable connection between him and Felicity was temporary and meaningless. Their first kiss had been incredible, and each subsequent embrace was both briefer and more desperate than the last, as if the less they allowed themselves, the more they tried to take.

Today, he intended to prove to Felicity that they could be so much more than colleagues.

He suspected she sensed it too. Not just because of the kisses. Anyone could kiss someone else without it meaning anything more than mere sexual desire.

But because she'd agreed to a picnic. His blood hummed with anticipation. This would be their first rendezvous outside of a smithy. No agenda, no apprentices, just the two of them seeing where this might go without a carriage standing between them.

If she put in an appearance.

Giles pulled his pocket watch from his waistcoat. Although it seemed like hours had passed, the hands of the clock showed barely five minutes past noon. Granted, Grosvenor Square was but a mile from his Oxford Street smithy. Just because Giles had been standing outside since ten minutes to twelve did not mean Felicity had even left—

One of the passing hackneys pulled to a stop directly in front of the smithy.

Please don't be a new customer, Giles prayed. *Please don't be a new customer.*

The door opened to reveal a faceless figure wearing the limpest, floppiest, least visually practical bonnet in all the world.

His heart leaped and he rushed forward to meet the carriage.

"I'm going to be very upset if that straw monstrosity is hiding someone other than my stable lass," he murmured as she placed her hand into his.

He felt, rather than saw, her smile.

She lifted up the brim of her hat to reveal twinkling brown eyes. "I missed you, too."

Those four simple words electrified him to his toes. They'd just seen each other the day before, yet he knew exactly what she meant. It didn't matter whether she was out of his sight for ten minutes or ten hours—she never left his mind.

Rather than help her down from the hackney, he swung the basket onto the seat across from her and hoisted himself into the carriage to give the driver the direction to St. James's Park.

Felicity glanced over at Giles in surprise. "I'd hoped we might be taking Baby."

"I worried you'd think her too recognizable. Besides," he said with narrowed eyes, "if I let you touch Baby, you'll never climb back down to have a picnic."

She inclined her head. "Fair."

The brim of her hat fell back over her face.

Giles undid the ribbon and stuffed the bonnet into the basket.

She leaned back against the seat and sighed. "I hate that thing."

"The basket?"

"The bonnet."

"Set it on fire," he suggested. "I'll help."

"It's unnecessary once I'm out of Mayfair," she admitted. "In these clothes and out of the usual haunts, I doubt I would be recognized by anyone but my own brother. But I still need the bonnet to escape Grosvenor Square."

Giles's jaw tightened. She could not risk being seen because she intended to keep her place in high society, not lower herself to publicly gadding about town on the arm of a blacksmith. His mere presence would ruin her reputation. He ought not to forget it.

He lowered his gaze to the picnic basket. Perhaps a romantic afternoon would change nothing at all. Days from now, the race would be over and that would be that.

Then again, she had eagerly agreed to today's outing. Disguised, so as to be unrecognizable to her peers of course, but at least she was here.

The next move was up to Giles.

When the hackney deposited them at a far less trafficked garden than Hyde Park, Giles picked up the basket with one hand and offered the other to Felicity.

She curled her fingers about his elbow and smiled. "Where to?"

"I'll show you." He escorted her deep along a rarely travelled footpath that led to one of his favorite little clearings.

He loved St. James's Park. His family had visited frequently when Giles was a child, and even now that he was the only one who still wandered through nature, he still came sometimes to recapture the feeling of doing absolutely nothing at all. Just lying on his back, eyes closed, rose-scented breeze rustling his hair, warm sunlight on his face, taking a moment to enjoy nature.

Felicity sent a worried gaze up at the sky. "I hope it doesn't rain."

"It won't," he replied.

This morning's storm clouds were off on the horizon. The weather should remain clear for their picnic.

She sent him a teasing look. "Are you the master of London weather, as well?"

"I'm the master of not caring two figs about the rain," he answered. "I didn't come here for the weather. I came for the company. And the kisses."

Her cheeks flushed prettily, and she gave him a soft kiss before swinging her gaze back to the gorgeous wooded path widening before them.

Giles had come to this special spot thousands of times with his family or on his own, but he had never brought a woman before. He watched Felicity from the corner of his eye as they stepped into the clearing.

Her eyes lit with wonder and she dropped her hand from his arm to clasp her fingers to her chest.

"This is beautiful!" She flung her arms wide and spun around, then turned to face him. "How did you find this?"

"This is where my father brought my mother when they started courting." Giles held a finger to his lips as if imparting a secret. "According to legend, nothing more scandalous occurred than a couple of chaste kisses."

"Good God." Felicity gasped in faux shock. "Anything but chaste kisses!"

He nodded gravely. "Unchecked licentiousness at its worst. Oh, and he did propose marriage here. So there is *that* precedent."

He expected Felicity to recoil at the implication that a courtship was underway. Instead, her gaze softened.

"How did he know she would say yes?"

"He didn't." Giles set the basket in a shady nook near some wildflowers. "That's why he brought her here. He hoped surrounding her with beauty would give him an advantage."

"Did it?"

"Definitely. Over the course of a summer, he procured two chaste kisses and one love of a lifetime. An unquestionable win." Giles spread a soft woolen blanket over the green spring grass and motioned for Felicity to join him.

She settled herself beside him. "How long have they been married?"

"Thirty-five years next month." He pulled cheese and fruit from the basket. With his folding pen knife, he began slicing bite-sized pieces onto a little platter.

"That's a long time," she said wistfully.

"To be married?"

"To have one's parents."

He looked up at her, his gut twisting in sympathy. He'd meant the story to be a romantic one; not a boast about what he had, and she did not.

"I know I'm fortunate," he said quietly. "I'm

grateful every single day. I'm sorry your parents are no longer with you."

"I don't remember them," she admitted after a long moment. "I try, but it's just… All I ever had was Cole. There was no time to sit around feeling sorry for ourselves."

Giles doubted that was entirely true. He knew from experience that a person was perfectly capable of being hard at work whilst grieving tragedy at the same time. Felicity's childhood could not have been easy.

"I'm glad your father was the sort who brought his son on picnics." Her expression was pensive. "There's nothing Cole and I wouldn't do for each other. That's why I know about carriages. We spent our childhoods working at a forge."

He tucked a stray curl behind her ear. "I've no doubt you were a deuce of an apprentice."

"By the time I was ten, I told everyone who would listen that I was going to be a blacksmith one day," she confessed with a self-deprecating smile. "How about you? Did you always want to be a coach smith?"

"Very much so," he answered. "My family would not have disowned me if I'd wished to be a butcher or a chemist instead, but for me there was never any question. I was born to it."

His family had never been rich, but they had always believed in each other and in him.

"Have you always wanted to be a duchess?"

he asked, thinking of her list. "Or a countess or a marchioness?"

She wrinkled her nose. "No. For so long, I was too worried about today to think about tomorrow. That all turned on its head when Cole inherited a dukedom. Suddenly there was a future to worry about. All I can do is make the best choices I can."

Giles wanted a happy, loving marriage like his parents had. Joy and contentment for thirty-five years and counting.

"Have you considered," he asked carefully, "the possibility of a love match?"

"Love doesn't buy bread." Felicity's dark eyes were haunted. "I refuse to raise a family in poverty, and I intend to lift as many other children up from that mire as I can. I'll marry whichever man whose advantages can create the most good."

Giles handed her a plate of fruit in silence. He did not find fault with her goals to improve children's futures. He shared them. They were just following two different paths to do so.

The big heart he admired so much was the reason she would never let herself see him as anything but a temporary diversion. He could offer love, but she was not seeking it. He lacked the high society pedigree required for his name to be added to her list.

Yet he could not help but wish there was

some way to convince her to see him as some-thing more.

"I wish you'd let me work on Baby," she said as she popped a grape into her mouth.

He finished off the last apple slice. "You'll never work on Baby."

"I saw you race," she said. "I could help."

"I *won*," he reminded her. "Handily, you might recall."

"But wouldn't it be splendid to leave your competitors behind in an even *bigger* cloud of dust?" she insisted, brown eyes sparkling. "I could shave at least thirty seconds off your time."

"No one would know." He lifted his pocket watch from his waistcoat pocket. "Most time-pieces don't display seconds."

"*You* would know," she said confidently. "The only reason you aren't saying yes is be-cause it would wound you to admit that the Curricle King might have missed a trick or two."

A slow smile threatened to take over his face. There was indeed a trick or two that it would wound him not to take advantage of. And it had nothing to do with races on Rotten Row.

"Very well," he said. "But a favor for a fa-vor. Right here. Right now."

Her eyes widened in alarm. "W-what kind of favor?"

"I'll neither ask for your hand nor for your

virginity," he assured her. At least, not without her enthusiastic consent.

Her frown deepened. "Then what do you want?"

A chance.

He stood up and held out his hand. "A waltz."

"A waltz?" she repeated in confusion as she placed her hand in his.

He pulled her to her feet and led her to the center of the soft grass.

She could not invite him into her world, like he'd invited her into his, but perhaps here among the trees and the birds and the flowers, they could create a private world to share with each other.

He began to dance.

She fit in his arms perfectly. As though they belonged together beneath the dappled sun. As though their entire lives had led to this moment, to this space, to the joy of each other's arms.

"You *can* waltz," she said in surprise, then blushed. "I didn't mean—"

"You did mean," he said with faux sternness. "Almack's isn't the only place with music, you know."

"You're right," she said softly. "I can feel the music in my soul, right here in the park."

He'd been referring to Vauxhall Gardens, but her quiet admission grabbed him by the heart. There was music all around. The rustle of leaves, the babble of a stream, the warble of a starling.

Like her, he could feel it in his soul.

He wanted her to be proud of him, wanted her to be happy *with* him. Not just in occasional stolen moments, but for—

"I should go," she said with reluctance. "I'm to have a fitting for a new gown."

"All right," he said, and meant it. But his lips had other plans.

She was already in his arms; close enough to kiss. All he had to do was close the distance between them.

Nothing on this earth could keep his mouth from hers.

Her tongue tasted like sweet red grapes and her skin smelled of springtime. With every kiss, her lips became more familiar and more impossible to resist. It was as though their mouths belonged together, their bodies, their hearts.

How could he convince her that what she felt was important, too?

CHAPTER 8

Felicity tucked a fresh rag into the waistband of her trousers and returned to her task of reseating new wheels. Now that Giles had allowed her to tinker with his most treasured possession, she was determined to prove herself worthy of his trust.

They were alone in his smithy, working on each other's carriages in a companionable silence intermittently broken by a technical question or a teasing comment about the other's obsession with cast tapered sleeves or the like.

Felicity couldn't remember passing a more delightful morning in quite some time.

When her brother had unexpectedly inherited, his reaction had been the exact opposite of hers. Cole never wanted to lay eyes on a forge or a slitting chisel ever again.

It wasn't that he believed himself above hard work, now that he possessed a title. He'd had to work harder than most to make top marks at Oxford, and he applied that same diligence and energy to both the House of Lords and his tavern.

To Cole, entering a smithy felt like failure. It smelled of poverty and angry tears and made his stomach twist with remembered hunger.

But Felicity did not remember the time when they'd lived with their parents in a tiny cottage outside London where the meals were simple but could be counted upon, along with the hugs and the smiles and the laughter.

To her, the smithy had meant warmth and camaraderie and a place to belong. It had meant being useful, being needed. "Little Felix" was a favorite, which only made her love the other lads all the more. *They* were the first home she could remember. The first time she had family other than Cole to count on.

Leaving them had been hard. Not just because she'd had to go from Little Felix to Lady Felicity, but because she'd had to learn to navigate an entirely new world.

Swage blocks were easy. Minuets were hard. Embroidery was impossible.

But she'd tried her damnedest, and somehow, she'd muddled through. High Society was her new home now. She had to remember that.

"Want more lemonade?" came Giles's voice from the other side of the shop.

She leaned an elbow on the tug stop. "What happened to the lemon tarts I ordered?"

"Kitchen's that way." He gestured toward the far door, then dropped back to the felloes. "Make a double batch. I'm peckish."

She laughed under her breath as she tested the security of a nut flange. The last thing Giles would expect was for her to take him up on his offer, and march into his kitchen to whip up a batch of fruit tarts.

He *did* expect her to do every bit as expert a job, when it came to spoiling Baby, as he and his father had done before her. His faith meant more to her than a thousand sonnets.

Not that she was in the market for love poems, she reminded herself. Just because she felt as much at home in Giles's smithy as her own did not mean it was ever going to *be* her home.

It just meant she had to enjoy every minute of their time together because she'd never again have moments like these to share.

She couldn't even enter her own brother's tavern without destroying her reputation in the process, much less pursue an eyebrow-raising friendship with a coach smith.

Even if he could waltz like an angel and gave kisses more tempting than the devil himself.

Giles poked his head over the footrest. His

handsome, irresistible smile made her pulse flutter anew. "I really am peckish."

"And I'm really not making lemon tarts," she said with arched brows.

Truth was, she didn't know how. If she did, she'd be tempted to bake a dozen every day, just to have an excuse to spend more time with him.

He tossed his apron onto the closest clear surface. "Come on. Let's go get some tea."

Her pulse leapt. Go…in? Inside his private quarters?

Felicity's stomach growled right on cue. Whether she was hungry for tea or more of Giles's drugging kisses remained to be seen.

Probably both.

She placed her apron beside his and followed him to the rear door.

Tea was not courtship, she reminded herself. Tea was something everyone drank. It meant nothing at all.

Even if the butterflies in her stomach begged to differ.

She followed him down a stairwell leading to a pretty, private residence facing the opposite street. It was clean, orderly, homey, just like his shop.

Unlike his shop, neither customers nor young apprentices were likely to wander in off the streets.

Here… anything could happen.

"I like your rooms," she said shyly.

"Do you?" he asked with obvious surprise. "I feel like it's missing some frescoes and gilt, and humble marble flooring."

"It's missing lemon tarts," she reminded him. "You can't eat marble flooring."

"I've never tried," he told her with wide eyes. "Does Almack's serve that with a little salt, or a dollop of French sauces?"

"Aren't you supposed to be cooking?" she grumped. "Mix some gold dust in my tea."

"I *knew* there was something I meant to pick up at market." He kissed the tip of her nose, then led her to a sunny parlor with a large window and cozy chairs. When she was settled, he rang a bell pull.

A fresh-faced maid immediately appeared. "Yes, sir?"

Felicity blinked. She shouldn't be surprised Giles had a maid. Who else would be fixing his meals and pressing fresh trousers for lady colleagues? He was far too busy to deal with such minutia himself. His time was better spent in carriage houses and on racing tracks.

Besides, Cole's list of approved suitors exclusively named men richer than Croesus, and they were all Giles's clients. If what her brother was paying him was anything to go by, Giles could afford a far more extensive staff than half the fortune-hunters at Almack's.

No wonder his home was far more elegant than she'd imagined.

"Just realizing untitled men can live comfortably, too?" he asked dryly.

Her cheeks heated.

"In my defense," she explained, "I've never known any who did. First I was incredibly poor and had nothing, and then I was incredibly rich and had everything. I never had a chance to experience having *some* of the things."

"I don't have 'some' of the things," Giles said as he settled into a comfortable sofa to her left. "I have all the things I care about. The things I appreciate most cannot be purchased."

A man who already had everything had no need for anything—or anyone—else.

There was no room for her. Not in his house, not in his smithy, not in his life. She should be glad. It should make walking away all the easier. And yet the thought of doing so ripped a hole in her chest.

She bit her lip. "Is there nothing else you want?"

Rather than answer, he looked away. The maid was just arriving with a tray laden with tea service and sandwiches.

"Allow me to pour this time," Felicity said.

Giles held out a palm in acquiescence.

"Pour fast," he warned, "else I might eat all the sandwiches while you dally."

"A lady never dallies when it comes to tea," she assured him.

Indeed, they didn't speak another word until every crumb was gone.

"You're not the only one who started with little and ended with a lot," he said as he collapsed back against his chair with a sated sigh.

Her heart thumped. The stiff-necked denizens of the ton would consider anything less than a palace to be an unfortunate hovel, but Felicity intimately understood how Giles felt. She just hadn't realized they shared that, too.

"You haven't always lived here?" she asked in surprise.

"I used to live there." He gestured back toward the entrance. "On the other side of that door is another set of rooms, above the original smithy. That's where my parents live."

Felicity blinked. That meant Giles's "rooms" spanned half the block.. and his parents' rooms spanned the other half.

"How did you afford it?" she asked.

Not a question one asked in polite society, but she and Giles were not currently in polite society. They were two people who had once intimately known the value and loss of every half-penny.

"Racing," he answered simply. "As it turns out, the risk-taking business is far more lucrative than the horseshoe-plating business."

This did not surprise Felicity at all. Not anymore, that was.

When she and Cole attempted to join society, they had both been appalled at the staggering sums wagered for no apparent reason. *I say my dog has bigger paws than your dog. The next person who walks through the door will be wearing a feathered cap. I bet my ancestral home that the next card I turn over will be the Jack of Diamonds.*

Cole had never wagered a farthing until he was invited to participate in the races. Coddled aristocrats might know everything there was to know about purchasing fine thoroughbreds and fancy coaches, but Felicity and Cole knew what it meant to be the ones taking care of them.

Her brother wasn't nearly the whip or the daredevil that Giles was—Cole only accepted dares he was certain he could win—but if the offer to race for money had been made to them twelve years ago, back when their long hours at the smithy was the closest they could come to securing any kind of a future...

She and her brother would have made the exact same choice Giles had.

A knife twisted in her chest as she wondered how different things might have been if she'd met Giles as equals, rather than as the sister of one of his aristocratic clients. Instead of running a charitable foundation funded by well-to-do philanthropists, she might be up to her elbows in axle grease, teaching boys and girls alike how to maintain a carriage. Instead of marrying a marquess, she'd...

She reached for Giles's hand. "I…"

Before she could continue, a white-haired woman with bright blue eyes burst into the parlor with arms laden with brown-paper parcels.

"Biscuits for the lads," she announced, then stopped dead at the sight of Felicity. "And I suppose this is the reason why I also brought lemon tarts?"

Felicity leaped to her feet to dip an elegant curtsey. When she realized she was still wearing trousers, she switched to an awkward bow halfway through.

"You baked lemon tarts for me?" she stammered in the hopes of distracting their visitor from whatever disaster of bent limbs Felicity had just performed.

"Oh, heavens no," the woman laughed. "I'm a terrible cook. These are from the bakery down the street. Obadiah sends his regards, by the way. His wagon has never been in better condition."

"Felicity," Giles said, "meet my mother, Mrs. Kenneth Langford. Mother, this is Felicity."

A lonesome stab of longing flashed through Felicity's heart. A deep yearning to be something more than a mere guest. To share Giles's home, his shop, his life. His wonderful mother, with her lemon tarts and warm, friendly smile.

"I won't interrupt for long," Mrs. Langford

said, her knowing eyes twinkling. "I just wanted to bring biscuits for his little helpers."

He kissed her cheek and reached for one of the parcels.

Mrs. Langford moved it out of reach. "None for you, sir. The biscuits are for your young apprentices, and that's final. If you'd like a lemon tart…" She handed a string-tied parcel to Felicity. "Then you'll have to work out your transaction with the lemon tarts' rightful owner."

Giles's mouth fell open.

The marvelous Mrs. Langford took the chair to Felicity's right. "May I have one?"

"You may have three." Felicity placed them in Mrs. Langford's palm, charmed. How she would love to have a mother like this! "Please say you can stay for more tea. You seem like a woman who must possess unlimited amusing stories about embarrassing anecdotes in Giles's past."

"Do I ever," Mrs. Langford agreed, popping a lemon tart into her mouth. "And I would be delighted to share every last one of them with you. First, there was the time at the Peerless Pool, when he—"

"*Mother…*" Giles began in warning.

Mrs. Langford waved his interruption away. "Oh, very well. It'll have to be next time, my dear. I'm afraid I cannot stay long." Her tone lowered as she turned to her son. "Might you come by soon… to…"

"Yes," he said quickly. "I haven't forgotten."

Felicity's smile faltered. The mirage shimmered and popped. Something was up, but their lives had nothing to do with her. That was not her family. This was not her home.

She didn't belong.

CHAPTER 9

"Colehaven!" cried a sea of voices, followed by an equally exuberant cry of, "Eastleigh!"

The sounds of laughter and clinking glasses filled the Wicked Duke tavern as its denizens cheered the arrival of the pub's owners and original namesakes. That the infamous "wicked dukes" were now happily married did not detract an iota from their charm.

This Season marked the tavern's ten-year anniversary. At first, London hadn't known what to think when two dukes purchased a property near the Haymarket and opened its doors to all walks of life.

Was it a fashionable pub? Not to the aristocrats who prized exclusivity and privilege above all things. Was it a popular pub, despite the absence of certain high-in-the-instep prigs? Absolutely.

Giles took a healthy swig of ale. Along

with Felicity's brother, this was where Giles had met the deep-pursed half of his clientele. He owed the success of both his smithy and his races to the men of this tavern.

There were women here, too, although the majority weren't of a class high enough to afford a horse, much less a carriage to pull behind it. Despite the owners' impressive titles, most rowdy pubs were not a place sophisticated society misses could frequent if they wished to keep their reputations intact.

He wished Felicity could join him here. The segregation of "fine" ladies from fallen ones had nothing to do with the Wicked Duke. If anything, the pioneering tavern did its best to welcome all and sundry. The problem was society's blatant double standard.

That must be what Felicity's entire life was like, he realized slowly. She disguised herself not because she was ashamed of the things she liked, but because she was never allowed to just be herself.

Being a lady sounded bloody awful.

A fresh tankard of ale clinked down on the table before him. "How's my curricle?"

Giles raised his glass to Colehaven's. "We'll win."

"I'm counting on it."

So was Giles. After every big race, the Wicked Duke always hosted a welcome reception for drivers and spectators alike. Keeping his reputation spotless and in the public eye was how Giles ensured future clients. He couldn't afford to lose a race—or to lose gentlemen like Colehaven as a client. Not if he wanted to keep all his apprentices and helpers.

"Is that Raymore?" Colehaven lifted his tankard from the table. "Excuse me for a moment. I need to talk with him about a matter for the House of Lords."

Giles inclined his head, but the duke was already gone. Lord business. Another reminder he didn't need of all the reasons his name had never been on Felicity's list.

He set down his tankard. There was still time to finish his ale, but Giles no longer was interested. He might not be a lord, but he, too, had an important meeting. Felicity would be coming to the smithy in an hour. If he left now, he could go home, change his clothes, perhaps have a quick jaunt down to the bakery in search of lemon tarts—

Felicity was already downstairs working on Baby when he walked through the door. His heart lightened.

She looked absolutely ravishing in lad's trousers.

Come to think of it, he had also begun to think she looked positively delectable in her nondescript day gowns and that horrid floppy bonnet.

Apparently, it was not the clothes he was

attracted to, but the talented, intelligent, bull-headed woman beneath.

He grinned at her. "You're early."

"I'm early." She smiled back. "There's biscuits on the counter."

"No lemon tarts?"

"I ate them." She arched a brow. "The most important rule of Giles's smithy is—"

"—arrive first," he finished. "No wonder you were an apprenticed smith at age twelve."

"Thirteen," she demurred, and set down her apron. "Ready to go?"

"I just got here," he reminded her, startled. "Also… didn't you say biscuits?"

"The biscuits will still be here half an hour from now."

"Where will *we* be?"

"Arriving home exhausted and exhilarated after taking the fastest curricle in London for a test drive. My brother's carriage is finally ready."

Giles stared at her.

He knew his line—anything along the lines of *what makes you think your curricle is faster than my curricle* would do—but his brain was still fracturing over the first words in her sentence.

Arriving home.

Home.

Home was here with him.

He swallowed hard, his heart racing too

erratically to think properly. Surely that was why he replied, "I'll get you a hat."

Her eyes widened.

"A proper hat," he added, grabbing one from a nail. "You'll go as one of my apprentices, not as my great-aunt Melba."

She leaped into the interior with the agility of a fawn.

"Remind me why I bother helping you in and out of hackneys?" he groused as he hoisted himself up into the seat beside her.

"Misplaced chivalry," she answered, then gestured toward the shaft tip. "I'm not the master of this smithy, but I think we might be missing a horse."

"I've got a horse," he assured her. "Several, in fact. But I needed to see how the height and weight difference would feel from the driver's perch."

"Decide faster," she begged as she clutched her hands to her chest and wriggled like a puppy. "I've been waiting a fortnight for this."

'You have not waited a fortnight," he said with a laugh. "You finished whatever you were just doing a scant moment ago, despite having begun this project a mere—"

Oh.

She didn't mean Project Curricle. She meant Project Giles-and-Felicity.

They'd met a fortnight ago. Colehaven's upcoming race was morning after next. This was their last chance for stolen moments of freedom like these. Giles swallowed hard.

"I'll summon the horses." He jumped to the floor. "Don't make any other modifications while I'm gone."

"Just my disguise," she promised, and began arranging a woolen scarf about the collar of a lad's jacket.

In no time at all, they were flying down Rotten Row with the wind in their faces and huge, silly smiles as each of them sent the other a *See? I told you so!* glance.

They could not have asked for a better day. The sky was cloudy enough to provide cover from the sun, yet clear enough to keep all threat of rain away. The hour was not late enough for the ton promenade to begin, nor so early as to interfere with other races.

It was as if Rotten Row was their own private Eden, a racing track made for no one else but Giles and Felicity.

...and a few assorted riders and pedestrians whose faces passed in such a blur as to be completely unrecognizable.

"Let me drive," she panted when they reached the other end.

He tightened his hold on the reins. "Not a chance."

"This is my brother's carriage. I've driven it a thousand times. You'll let me take it apart and rearrange Baby as I see fit, but you won't relinquish control of my family's curricle for a single moment, even on a wide, closed track with no other carriages?"

"You *are* a quick study," he said in awe. "It's like you can peer inside my mind."

She narrowed her eyes. "I know what you're thinking."

"Do you?" He hoped not.

Because what he was thinking was that the next time he was on this track, he'd be alone in this carriage… and after that, he'd never lay eyes on her again. They had less than forty-eight hours. He couldn't risk anything happening to her.

"It's just a test ride," she wheedled, batting her eyelashes with alarming velocity.

"Apprentices don't bat their eyelashes," he hissed.

"Don't they?" Her eyes widened. "Perhaps you don't know as many as you think you do."

"You're not driving," he said firmly. "I need this curricle to win a race. I'll buy you some other carriage and you can test ride in that. A nice, solid, coach-and-four. I'll have it here by tomorrow."

"I don't want something *boring*," she said in exasperation. "I want excitement. I could build my own chariot, just as fast and light on her wheels as Baby, if I wanted to."

"Go do it then," he suggested with amusement. "I'll wait here."

"I just want ten minutes," she begged. "I want to know what it feels like to be fast and free and… *happy*. Not on my countless midnight rides alone. I want to feel that way with *you*."

How was he supposed to say no to that?

He handed over the reins. "One minute. A single second more, and I'll snatch those reins from your greedy hands."

"Pocket watches don't track seconds," she reminded him, and then they were off.

The expression of unadulterated joy on her face brought an equally irrepressible grin to his own. His heart gave a little dance.

Flying down this track made him feel indescribably alive. Truly present in the curricle, in the race, in the universe. It was power and powerlessness, freedom and holding on tight. No other feeling could ever compare.

He'd never had someone he could share that magic with before. Someone who would understand. Someone who felt it, too.

Felicity was every inch as much a daredevil as he was. She was confident and unexcitable, fearless and strong.

And she was right. There was no one else he wished to have beside him.

He was supposed to be the best in the game, but all he could think about was changing his sole proprietorship to a partnership. He and Felicity would make an unstoppable team. Privately and publicly.

Only when they reached the opposite end of the track did she hand back the reins. Her eyes were shining, her breath was shaky, her face was flushed—she was feeling *energized*. Exactly like Giles felt after every big race.

And every time he kissed Felicity.

"Come on," he said. "There's someone I want you to meet."

In minutes, they were back at the smithy.

Felicity laughed. "I met your mother yesterday, so you must mean…"

"The best father in all the world?" Giles asked. "The rumors are true. Walter Langford sets the standard."

Felicity raised a playful finger. "Don't you find it a teeny bit selfish to have the best mother in the world *and* the best father?"

I'll share them with you, Giles wanted to say, but didn't.

First, they needed to meet.

And then they needed to choose each other.

Felicity paused by the folding screen as they crossed through the smithy to the rear door.

"Just a moment," she said. "Let me change into a dress first."

He shook his head.

"No time?" she asked in surprise.

"No need for costumes," he answered. "He wants to meet *you*, not your disguise."

She swallowed visibly. "Don't you think it's a teeny bit selfish to have the best mother, the best father, and also be the best person I have ever met?"

He blinked. "For letting you wear trousers?"

"For letting me be me," she whispered.

Before he could answer, Mother swung open the door with enthusiasm. "Could you smell biscuits baking all the way from the street?"

"I thought you didn't bake," Felicity stammered.

"True." Mother hauled her into the apartment. "There are no biscuits. Which means you two are here to see *me*."

"And Father," Giles added.

Mother paused for such a slight moment, no one would have noticed it but him.

"And Father," she agreed. "He's in the sitting room. Come."

Father was always in the sitting room. Staring out the window at the people passing below was one of the few pastimes he had left. He rarely allowed himself to be wheeled anywhere else while he was awake.

"Good God," Felicity said in shock when she entered the room. "You didn't tell me your father was even more handsome than you."

"You're the first one he's brought over," Father said in his low, shaky voice. He clucked his tongue. "Can you stay for a minute?"

"I can stay for hours." Ignoring the wingback chairs, she dragged a footstool next to

Father's wheeled chair so she could sit next to him at the window. "Giles really hasn't brought friends up to meet you before?"

"Oh, *friends*," Father scoffed. "Sure, plenty of them. Giles has more friends than a dog has fleas. But he's never before brought a..." Father lowered his voice. "Forgive me. Was it Lord Felix or Lady Felicity?"

She burst out laughing and glared over her shoulder at Giles. "You are the very worst."

"You said I was the best!" he protested.

"I changed my mind," she said. "Female prerogative."

"Then it's Lady Felicity," his father said with a smile. "I'm very pleased to meet you."

"Believe me," she answered. "The pleasure is mine."

Over his father's trembling shoulder, Felicity's gaze met Giles's. He understood the questions in her eyes.

She didn't wonder why his father was in a wheeled chair. The rhythmic muscle contractions and palsied hands, the soft, slurred speech, the bit of drool on his stiff jaw—Father's ill health was unmistakable.

Nor was she wondering why all of Giles's friends were familiar sights in this parlor. Giles was proud of his mother and father, and with good reason. His parents were clever and droll, and caring and friendly. Who wouldn't wish to take tea with them?

The question in Felicity's eyes was why he

had brought her to meet them.

"She wants embarrassing stories," Giles's mother prompted her husband.

Giles closed his eyes. "Mother—"

"We have so many stories," came his father's shaky voice. "There was the time you drank too much sherry when the rector was over for supper, and you started to sing that bawdy ditty—"

"Not embarrassing stories about *me*," Mother interrupted quickly. "Embarrassing stories about our son."

"I like all stories." Felicity leaned back against the windowsill as though she had first row seats at the theater. "I can be here all night."

"I wish you would." Mother held a hand to her mouth to block her lips from Giles's view. "There really are biscuits, but Giles can't be trusted not to eat them all. Once we get him to go back to his quarters—"

"I'm standing right here," he said dryly. "And I know where you hide the biscuits."

Mother crossed her arms and let out an exaggerated sigh. *"Foiled."*

Too late, Giles realized the trap he'd set for himself. When he'd brought Felicity here, he'd been worried about her reaction, not his parents'. Of course it was love at first sight. Now that his parents had met her, they would want him to keep her. *Giles* wanted to keep her.

And Lady Felicity wasn't the keeping kind.

CHAPTER 10

The Everett ball was the biggest crush of the season, but Felicity's mind was a mile away. Specifically, the beautiful little clearing Giles had taken her to have their first waltz. It was hard to concentrate on chandeliers and orchestras when all she could think about was dancing in the grass with no music but their own and the scent of flowers in the air.

Her pulse fluttered. That day in the park had been perfect. Dappled sun, light breeze, Giles's delectable kisses that made her tingle all the way to her toes. Every kiss, every caress, made her wish the moment could last forever. As though his arms were where she had been born to stay.

But it wasn't just his romantic inclination to waltz anywhere they happened to be. She could show up at Giles's smithy as who she was, dressed how she pleased, and he would just smile that seductive smile and hand her a lathe. Or perhaps a lemon tart and a fresh cup of tea.

And racing! Handling the curricle with him at her side instead of sneaking out for lonesome midnight rides had been the most free, joyful, exhilarating moment of her life. They had felt like a team. Like they belonged together.

Of course his parents were perfect. She'd assumed as much after getting to know Giles, but they'd confirmed her suspicions in the best way possible.

The idea of never seeing them again, of never finding out exactly how bawdy the ditty was that Mrs. Langford sang to the rector after too much sherry, was almost more than Felicity could bear.

She would *miss* them. And she already missed Giles. Tomorrow morning was the big curricle race. There was no time to see him before, no chance of running into him after…

Unless…

What if there was some way she could keep him? Not as a carriage consultant or secret friend, but as something more? Her heart thumped. What was she saying? Marriage? Giles hadn't asked, likely because they both knew Cole would never approve a match between his sister and a coach smith.

Nor would running off to Gretna Green solve all their problems. Marrying Giles would sacrifice more than her relationship with her brother. It would limit future charitable works. Although she wouldn't be rescinding her vow altogether, a non-peer marriage would compromise how much she was able to achieve.

She could still help children at the smithy, but without the backing of a well-funded charitable foundation, she wouldn't be able to save as many.

Would doing her best be enough?

"Here he comes," Cole murmured.

For a dizzy, unreal moment, Felicity half-expected to see Giles emerge from the Everett's crowded dance floor.

Instead, her eyes met across the room with Lord Raymore, who smiled just before being waylaid by some friends.

A reprieve. Felicity's shoulders relaxed. Perhaps he hadn't been heading this way after all.

But wasn't that what she wanted? Wasn't he the answer to a lifelong prayer?

"He's a good man," Cole said gruffly.

She nodded. "I know."

He ticked all the boxes on both their lists. Wealthy and titled enough for Cole to believe he was making the best possible match for his sister. Kindhearted and socially empathetic enough for Felicity to know he'd make a wonderful ally in her plans to divert the ton's resources toward the people who needed it most.

A dream come true. She swallowed hard.

"We're on the child labor reform committee together," Cole continued.

Felicity nodded again. She didn't trust herself to speak.

"When I saw him yesterday at the Wicked Duke, I thought he wanted to talk about the new initiatives he'd proposed in the House of Lords." Cole gave Felicity a conspiratorial wink. "He wanted me to know he held you in the highest regard and wanted my blessing to find out if you felt the same."

Her heart stopped.

"You did it," Cole whispered. "I could not be prouder of you. He's a lowly marquess, rather than a duke—"

Felicity smiled weakly.

"—but I can sleep happy knowing you've made an incredible match with a husband who will treat you like a lady and give you every advantage High Society has to offer." Cole's eyes shone with brotherly love. "Raymore will have no problem signing a betrothal contract with a charitable works clause. He'd probably insist upon it. Just imagine what the two of you can do!"

She *was* imagining. She'd been imagining this very thing since she and her brother were two urchins covered in dirt and axle grease. The dream of *someday* had kept them alive.

The last thing she'd ever do was let her

brother down. He was happily married now, but before that, he'd spent years sacrificing for Felicity. The first promises they ever made had been to each other. The kinds of lives they'd live if the opportunity ever arose.

This was opportunity rising. She couldn't let Cole's sacrifices be for nothing.

"There you are," said a cheerful voice. "The loveliest lady in the ballroom. Lady Felicity, may I have this dance?"

Of course he could. Lord Raymore was the reason she was *in* this ballroom.

She couldn't let herself forget.

At her brother's encouraging smile, Felicity gave the marquess her hand and let him lead her before the orchestra.

The music began. A waltz.

Her shift itched. The stagnant air was unbearable and her layers of skirts far too heavy. She wished she were wearing trousers. No, she wished she were wearing breeches. They were half as long as trousers, and in this ballroom soup, she'd take any relief she could get.

Except there were no more breeches in her future, were there? Just thousands more balls just like these, her clothing growing stiffer and less airy every year as she aged into a respected old matron.

A respected old matron with the bottomless purses of the ton at her beck and call.

There were children out there with no fresh clothing at all. Felicity had once been one of them. "Forced to marry a rich marquess" was hardly an impressive sacrifice if it meant keeping her vow to do everything in her power to help others.

"Your brother tells me you've a passion for charitable works."

This particular personality quirk had sent half a dozen spendthrift suitors running. Lord Raymore's eyes were kind; his voice interested. He wasn't disappointed. He was delighted.

"I'd like to start a foundation." Her legs wobbled nervously. She'd never admitted her goal aloud to anyone but Cole and Giles. *Donating spare coin* was a far cry from *running a charitable organization.* "I've never managed one before, but..."

Lord Raymore didn't scoff. He smiled instead. "As it happens, I have a bit of experience in that regard myself. The Children's Circulating Library now runs like clockwork, but in the early days—"

"*You're* the anonymous benefactor behind the library?" Felicity blurted.

Hester donated to that cause. So did Lady Donnell, Lady Mortram, the Earl of Fortescue, and countless others.

Lord Raymore's cheeks tinged with pink. "Slightly less anonymous now that I've told *you* my secret, but yes. That's one of my projects. I dislike being in the public eye, but I am passionate about improving the lives of children. Tell me about the foundation you'd like to start."

The words tumbled from Felicity's mouth of their own accord. Raymore listened attentively, interrupting only with insightful questions and thoughtful suggestions.

If she married him, there would be no need to spend the rest of her life wheedling every penny out of him. The marquess was not only already willing to do everything Felicity dreamed, but also possessed the means and status to make the rest of the ton follow his lead.

This was it. Mission accomplished. Success was in sight.

So why did it feel like her heart was breaking?

*D*awn. The air was crisp, the heavy sky was streaked with orange, and Rotten Row was as crowded as Vauxhall Gardens on balloon launch day.

This was it. The big race.

Despite having been on her feet for the past twenty hours, Felicity was wide awake.

Six immaculate curricles were inching toward the starting line, two-by-two. As prior champion, Giles was in the final row next to Silas Wiltchurch. The chariots might have to bank slightly off-track in order to pass each other, but no one was worried about the grass. Today was about winning.

Most of the spectators swarmed near the waiting curricles, in the hopes of shouting words of encouragement—or good-natured insults—to the drivers.

Felicity had chosen a spot twenty yards past the starting line. She had no desire to glimpse Giles sitting still in a stationary carriage. That wasn't his natural state. She wanted to witness him flying down the track, moving from last to first in the blink of an eye, to the roar of an exuberant crowd.

Not to mention that somewhere in this packed crowd, her brother was here to monitor the outcome of his wager. Felicity had made certain to blend with the crowd on the opposite side of the track. Her brother might indulge her eccentricities by allowing Felicity to tinker safely out of public sight, but Cole would kill her if he knew she was out and about unchaperoned. Dressed as a lad or otherwise.

If the first race she'd watched had been capital fun, this one was twice as exciting. These weren't any old carriages out for a Hyde Park jaunt. There was her brother's carriage. The curricle Felicity had worked on for the past fortnight.

And the appointed driver was *her* Giles. The man whose bare hands had, on more than one occasion, been deep in her hair as he claimed her mouth. Not this morning, unfortunately. She was dressed as a lad in trousers, not his great-aunt Melba—neither of whom it would have been appropriate to kiss in public.

But there would be no more kisses in their future. Felicity shouldn't even be here now, not with a marriage proposal from Lord Raymore on the line. No, not a mere proposal on the line, but her charitable foundation, and the lives of countless children. *That* was Felicity's future.

This race was goodbye.

Giles would not be shocked to learn she intended to accept the marquess's suit. She'd never hid her plans from him. They'd known where each other stood from the beginning. What they'd shared was magical, but temporary. They'd walked into it with open eyes and would walk away the same way.

Boom.

At the crack of the starting pistol, all six curricles were off.

Felicity's heart lurched. Every inch of her brimmed with pure, unadulterated joy whenever she was near Giles, even if she could only watch from the shadows.

A wet droplet splashed on her nose, and she cast her gaze skyward. The dark clouds overhead had been spitting occasional raindrops, but it didn't look like it would storm quite yet.

Not that Giles would need that much time to annihilate the competition. No one could hold a candle to his skill at the reins.

As the carriages thundered past, one, two, three, four, five, *six*—there he was!—Giles turned his head at the last second as if he sensed Felicity's presence despite the cover of the crowd.

He couldn't see her. Could he?

Giles winked.

A giddy laugh threatened to spill from her chest. He *had* seen her! She was at her most invisible, dressed in trousers in the least likely spot of a very large crowd, and he had found her as easily as if their souls were entwined.

Was it any wonder she'd fallen hopelessly, irreversibly in love with this maddening, wonderful man? Goodbye or not, as soon as he won this race, she'd be tempted to sail straight into his arms and kiss him senseless. He was—

In trouble.

Barely fifty yards past the starting line, Silas Wiltchurch drove his horses into Giles's path in a bald attempt to force his chaise out of the running. Horses reared in alarm as flying puffs of dirt and the crunch of wheels rent the air.

Any closer, and wheels would touch wheels, risking the safety of both carriages— and the lives of the drivers.

Wiltchurch veered toward Giles again, this time even more recklessly. Giles would either crash into the driver ahead—or a tree to the right.

Giles swerved his curricle off the road and onto the grass, expertly threading the narrow distance between the track and the tree trunk.

It might have worked, had a low branch not dipped directly in his path.

Giles threw up his arms just in time to prevent the thick, knobby branch from pulverizing his face.

It got his arm instead.

Dust and blood went flying, the curricle stopped dead in its tracks, and Silas Wiltchurch—

Continued on as if nothing had happened, gleefully speeding up to overtake the next carriage in line.

"Bloody villain," Felicity hissed under her breath as she plowed through the crowd, sprinting toward Giles as fast as she could.

"Check the horses," he gasped the moment he saw her.

"Your *arm*," she replied in horror, ignoring the carriage. Her lungs seized. The sleeves of his jacket were flayed open. Patches of red spread beneath. She couldn't breathe.

"My silk racing shirt didn't tear," he said. "I'm bruised and bloody, but fine. *Check the horses.*"

He still meant to *win*, she realized in awe. Heart racing, she ran to the horses. They were unhurt, but agitated. They calmed at her familiar touch. In a trice, they seemed ready to fly back onto the track and trounce Silas Wiltchurch.

As much as Felicity supported such a plan, safety came first. She hurried to the other side of the curricle, where the two wheels had almost come into contact. Filthy, but no fractures. The carriage was still sturdy and well-seated. Wiltchurch had failed.

"Everything's fine," she called up, then frowned at the sight of Giles's swelling arm. "Are you certain you can drive?"

"*Yes*," he said firmly. Then, "Maybe."

She grabbed the splinter bar and hauled herself up into the curricle beside him.

"What are you doing?" he hissed.

She grabbed the reins from his lap and jerked her head toward the side of the track, where a crowd was forming. "Meet me at the finish line."

"Be safe." He clutched his arm to his chest and managed to leap to the ground. "And *win!*"

The crowd echoed his shout.

She could do this. Felicity knew these horses; knew this carriage. She would win or die trying.

"Yah!" she yelled, and nearly fell back against the seat as the horses leaped back onto the track and took off after the others as if they wanted Silas Wiltchurch to choke on their dust just as badly as she did.

Rage spurred them to speeds they'd never reached before.

Felicity had known Wiltchurch was a petty snob and a poor loser, but she'd never expected him to stoop to sabotage at the potential cost of human life. Not in front of all these witnesses. She would not let him get away with it.

Thunder shook the sky. She could barely hear it over the rumble of wheels and the roar of wind in her ears.

She wasn't driving. She was soaring.

This was who she was. A demon in trousers, here to make him rue the day he'd endangered the life of the man she loved. They were no longer horse and driver, but an unstoppable bullet speeding through the air faster than the eye could see. But it wasn't enough. They'd lost too many precious seconds.

Cold rivulets of rain streaked across her face as she reached the first carriage.

She wouldn't beat Giles's time from the last race.

He'd turned around before the others had even neared the end of the track, and today it was Felicity who was watching the others turn and speed toward her, then disappear.

But she'd caught up; or close enough. She was now only a few yards behind the next curricle.

She made her turn at the end of the track and tore toward the finish line.

CHAPTER 12

Giles cradled his swollen arm to his thundering chest and stepped one foot back onto the dirt to squint down the track. Rain matted his hair, his clothes. The crowd tried to swarm him at once.

"Back away," he growled. "I'll answer your questions after the race."

He did not know whether their acquiescence was a testament to how much they revered him, or to their equal desire not to miss a single moment of whatever might happen next. His pulse raced with excitement and fear.

Giles had shown up this morning with the sole goal of winning a race, but now his heart was in his throat as he watched Felicity take his place. He wanted to win, but not at the expense of her safety. Yet she was fearless on the track.

They'd lost valuable time with the crash, the inspection, the bickering as to which one of them belonged behind the reins, but she was already closing the lost distance and was coming up fast on the curricle in second-to-last place.

The rain was coming down harder, but he blinked it away. Giles rarely watched a race from the sides. It was excitement and chaos and almost as much fun as being the one up in the driver's seat, racing for his life.

His heart swelled with pride as Felicity neatly passed the other carriage with a wide, safe berth.

He screamed his encouragement, his heart racing more wildly than the horses tearing down the track.

It would take a miracle to make it first to the finish line, but already this race would be the talk of the town for months to come: Giles Langford, Curricle King, had handed the reins to an unknown lad when that insufferable Silas Wiltchurch had run him from the road.

And the unknown lad was catching up with the competition.

Lord Felix, indeed. Master of his carriage and keeper of his heart.

When she passed a second curricle, he let out a war whoop that was drowned by the equally hysterical reactions of the deafening crowd. His legs and fingers shook.

She was doing it. *She was doing it.*

Giles bounced on his toes despite the jarring pain to his arm. He was thrilled and terrified, slightly panicked and insanely proud.

Felicity wasn't mere competition. She was a master at the helm, an avenging goddess, an unstoppable force.

The nearer she drew to the finish line, the closer she came to Silas Wiltchurch. Giles didn't trust that blackguard as far as he could throw him.

But he'd trust Felicity with his life.

It had been past time for her to take the reins and finally do as *she* wished. Whatever that might be, he wouldn't stand in her way. He'd support her, come what may. That was what partners did.

Despite the rain and the accident and the spectators and the sprays of mud, she looked as calm and competent as ever. Her body was relaxed at the reins, and her face was smiling. The sight filled his chest with warmth.

Giles knew exactly what it felt like to fly high on a perch, overtaking competitor after competitor to the roar of an adoring audience.

He hadn't known it would bring him the same joy to watch Felicity experience that same rush. To share that sense of being one with God and nature, with curricle and horses, with the crowd.

No wonder she'd begged for the opportunity to take Baby down this track. Felicity was born for this. A natural.

She passed a third carriage, leaving only two more between her and the finish line.

Ice snaked through Giles's chest.

The finish line meant winning, but it also meant losing Felicity. She had commandeered his heart and taken him on the ride of a lifetime. Their partnership had always been temporary. This was the end.

Unless he did something about it.

They were meant for each other. He knew it; she must suspect the same. There was only one thing to do. His pulse jumped.

Ask her to marry him.

He had never quit anything just because there'd been a high chance of failure. He was in this race to win it.

Felicity passed a fourth curricle. Now it was just her and Silas Wiltchurch, less than two hundred yards from the end. Wiltchurch's fancy connections might let him get away with murder in Felicity's world, but here at the races, he was nothing but a petty blackguard. The crowd had been on Felicity's side from the moment she took the reins.

But she would need more than a cheering crowd to win. Wiltchurch was an insufferable, egotistical bully, but he was a ruthless driver in an exquisite carriage. He was used to winning and already had a head start. Giles could only stand helpless, his heart thundering as he watched.

Wiltchurch stuck to the center of the

track, weaving back and forth so as not to allow any space for passing him on either side.

But all that weaving cost him momentum. His fifty-yard lead was now a thirty-yard-lead, then twenty, then ten.

When Felicity went left, Wiltchurch went left to block her.

When Felicity went right, Wiltchurch went right to block her.

When Felicity tried the left again, Wiltchurch—

But she *wasn't* trying the left! It was a feint; meant to make her opponent overreact to a perceived threat.

It was all the opening she needed.

With a final burst, she rounded him on the right, the nose and neck of her horses crossing the finish line half a second before Wiltchurch's did the same. Giles's heart exploded.

Complete pandemonium.

The crowd erupted in screams and whoops, cheering delightedly because the villain had got exactly what was coming to him.

Giles's throat was already hoarse from all of his own yelling, and he took off running toward the finish line to sweep Felicity into his arms, trousers and all. She was his and they *had done it,* because they were a team and un-bloody-stoppable.

He couldn't wait to swing her around—

albeit with one arm—and kiss her, twirl her, dance with her, propose to her...

So where the devil *was* she?

Panting from exertion and pain, Giles stared in befuddlement at the Duke of Colehaven's empty curricle.

Felicity had been *right here*. Seconds ago. But now the only nearby person he recognized was—

The Duke of Colehaven.

Giles gulped at the duke's understandably stormy expression.

"Congratulations," he said, when the silence seemed to stretch indefinitely. "We won."

At this, the duke's face went purple.

"*You* were supposed to win," he snarled. "I paid *you* to race my carriage. Not to put... someone else... in harm's way."

Giles held up his wounded arm. "In the course of winning you the race, you might have noticed Silas Wiltchurch—"

"—is an insect whom I will deal with without remorse," the duke interrupted. "But he was not the man I hired, and trusted to protect—"

Giles pulled up straight.

"*My* partner," he enunciated, "should not be hidden and does not wish for anyone's uninvited protection. If he wishes to display his talents to the world, I am not fool enough to get in his way."

The duke opened his mouth.

Giles didn't back down. "I don't 'let' him do anything except be himself, and live the life he wishes. Blacksmith or emperor of England, it's not up to me."

"It is *not* up to you," the duke said coldly. "The race is over. You're done."

CHAPTER 13

Felicity hurtled through the crowd, heading not toward the celebrations but to the road.

Despite the joy thundering through her chest, she still could not quite credit that she'd won. No, *they'd* won! It didn't matter who held the reins. She could not have won without Giles, and he could not have won without her.

They were a team. The best team. As elemental and unstoppable as the rain soaking through her clothes.

She could hear the roar of the crowd behind her as she hurried away. She wished she could be in the thick of it. Wished she could do it again and again.

Wished she were standing next to Giles right this moment, not just to celebrate, but to check his arm, to kiss his lips.

Instead, her brother had been the first person she'd seen at the finish line. He'd plucked her from the carriage and spirited her from the track before the crowd had a chance to reach her.

And then threatened to deal with her fully the moment he returned home. Starting with burning her trousers and locking her in her chambers if that was what it took to keep her safe.

Felicity didn't want to be safe. She wanted to be... *free*. At least long enough to say goodbye to Giles in person. His absence from her life was already ripping a hole in her chest.

She burst from the trees and trudged down the street toward Grosvenor Square.

A hack pulled to the corner. "Need a ride, lad?"

Did she?

Grosvenor Square was two blocks away. Walking distance. Right back to a life of opulence and luxury, fine dresses and intractable rules. That was her future.

But it didn't have to start right now.

"Thank you." Felicity hauled herself into the hackney. "Langford smithy, please. On—"

"Oxford Street," finished the driver, and pulled out into traffic.

Felicity grinned to herself. Of course any hack driver worth his salt would know the Langford smithy. Giles had more loyal subjects than the Prince Regent.

When they arrived, Felicity tossed the driver an extra coin and leaped to the ground.

The smithy doors were closed tight. Giles must give his workers a free hour during a big race, in case they wished to take part in the festivities. It didn't matter. She wasn't here to work on carriages.

She walked around to the other side where the front-facing door to his residence stood and gave the knocker a smart rap.

After a moment, the door swung open to reveal a familiar face: the maid who had brought tea to Giles's parlor just a few days prior.

It felt like a lifetime ago.

"Come in," the maid gasped. "You're soaked! I'll have a hot bath and a fresh change of clothes sent up at once."

That sounded positively divine.

With gratitude, Felicity followed her to a previously unseen portion of Giles's home, where she was handed off to a second maid, who coddled and cooed over her even more than the first. She felt like a princess.

Or a victorious charioteer, home from battle.

Felicity groaned in pleasure as the hot bath soaked the tension from her tight muscles. The only thing missing was Giles.

Given the size of the crowd, he might not return for hours. That would give Felicity plenty of time to make herself more presentable and come up with the right words for her farewell speech.

Just because they had both always known goodbye was imminent, did not make saying the words any easier.

She wouldn't burden him with the knowledge that she loved him, but she wanted him to know how much their time together had meant to her. He had accepted her as who and what she was, without any attempt to make her fit some preconceived notion of what females were capable of.

That alone was swoonworthy, but she adored the rest of the package just as much. From the first time he—

The bedchamber door flew open.

It was not a maid with an armful of dry clothes, but the wet and bedraggled love of her life… who had never seen her naked. She gasped and covered her breasts with her arms, bracing herself for a wave of shame and awkwardness. It didn't come.

This was Giles. She could be herself with him in a bonnet or trousers or nothing at all. If this was the last time they'd see each other, only a fool would fail to take advantage of every opportunity fate bestowed upon them. Tomorrow, she could be a respectable lady.

Today belonged to her and Giles.

CHAPTER 14

*A*fter his conversation with her brother, Giles had not expected to see Felicity again. Let alone discover her in his bedroom. Wet. Naked.

She scooted to the other side of the bath and patted the water. "Come in. The water's fine."

He kicked the door shut and stalked over to her without taking off his clothes. If he removed so much as his cravat, all chance of restraint would be lost.

"I was worried sick about you," he growled.

"About me?" She rose to her feet and met his gaze at eye level. "I've been worried sick about *you.*"

Or would have, if meeting his gaze had not been delayed an irresistible second, as he took in the dripping, naked body standing in front of him.

She was not offering herself to him in

marriage. She might not have intended to offer herself to him at all. But here they were, and she was not shying away. She was leaning closer.

"Let me see your arm," she said softly.

"Arm?" he croaked.

"This one." She pried it from his chest and winced at the profusion of contusions and dried blood. "That's it. I'm killing Wiltchurch."

"I'm fine," Giles assured her.

Naval officers wore silk shirts beneath their uniforms because of the strength of the fabric during combat. Giles didn't expect to confront enemy soldiers, but a racing track was often a battlefield of its own. This hadn't been his first accident.

He held up his arm. "The bone's not broken. It'll be good as new in a week or two."

She stared at him doubtfully. "It doesn't look like it'll be good as new. It looks like somebody ought to accidentally shove Silas Wiltchurch in the Thames."

Giles fully intended to have it out with Wiltchurch. Publicly, in front of plenty of witnesses. Today, in fact. High Society might suffer fools, but Giles did not. He'd ensure the blackguard was never welcome in another race again.

He lifted his good hand to Felicity's cheek. "I've suffered worse. Mostly when my heart stopped, as I watched you drive away."

She leaned her cheek into his palm with a small smile. "I did it."

"You did it," he confirmed. "I wish I could swing you in my arms and dance you around this room like you deserve."

"There's a second option." She licked her lips. "A way to celebrate that requires very little dancing and even fewer clothes."

Giles knew he should dissuade her from this tack. Not because he didn't want to ravish her—she was voicing the exact thoughts he'd been having—but because he'd wanted it to mean *more*. Making love to Felicity should be the beginning, not the ending.

She touched a fingertip to his damp lapel. "You should get out of these wet clothes."

"I…" He glanced at her finger on his chest, then down to her naked body, and felt his self-control slipping away. "I'm not certain that's the wisest idea."

"Let me help." She plucked at his cravat. "For purely practical reasons. At least let me clean your arm."

He gave a tight nod. There. He would prove his arm was fine, they'd put their clothes back on, and that would be that.

Maybe.

She began to unfasten each button of his jacket, of his waistcoat, slowly, deliberately. He sucked in his stomach as her fingers stripped him a little barer with each pop of a button.

"I'll try not to hurt you," she murmured as she eased his ruined jacket from his wide shoulders and carefully off each arm. "But I can't promise not to."

He knew that. He'd known from the beginning. This moment was worth it.

"What I'm feeling isn't pain." He leaned into her touch despite himself. He couldn't help it.

This was what she wanted. This was what *he* wanted. There was no sense fighting it.

Once the jacket and waistcoat had been tossed aside, she stepped from the tub. "Now your shirt."

The cloud of white silk was up over his head and down onto the floor within seconds.

"You can't get in the water with your boots on." She knelt at his feet.

He yanked the closest footstool next to the tub and sat down hard.

She tugged off each boot, then each stocking, and pushed them toward the wall. "Stand up."

He locked his hands behind his back to keep from reaching for her.

She unbuttoned his fall with the same care she'd given his jacket and waistcoat, in slow, unhurried movements. One button. Two buttons. Three.

Even before she'd begun, the evidence of his arousal was clearly delineated against his fall. Having it stiff and hot in her hands, however, was a different experience entirely. He groaned and tried not to thrust into her fingers when she gave it a tentative stroke.

"Bath," he gasped and sank into the tub, hiding his lower half from view.

She knelt beside him, reaching in to inspect his wounded arm. Gently, she cleaned the broken skin with soap and a soft rag.

"See?" he managed. The arm was swollen and discolored, but not broken. He'd been very, very fortunate.

When she finished with his arm, she brought the soap and the warm cloth to the rest of his body. Neck, shoulders, chest, stomach, hips. When she reached her hand further beneath the water, he grabbed her wrist with his good hand before she made contact.

"Not yet," he growled.

Her eyes widened, then sparkled in anticipation. "That's a yes?"

"It was a yes the moment I walked through the door and saw you naked." He didn't bother making noises about her reputation. She had always lived two lives. The public one she admitted to, and the private one she kept to herself.

Today would be just another one of her secrets.

He handed her a towel and dried himself with another before crossing to his armoire.

He always kept fresh bandages handy in case of accidents. The silk had saved his arm from dirt and debris, but wrapping the injury would keep the scratches from infection and help calm the swelling.

Task complete, he turned to face Felicity. The towel he'd given her was twisted about her hair, rather than hiding her perfect body. What he wouldn't give to start every morning just like this.

"This is the moment," he said huskily, "when I ought to toss you over my shoulder and carry you over to that bed."

"And you can't? You poor dear." She gave a wicked smile. "You'll have to watch me walk to the bed on my own two feet and open my legs for you all by myself. We're a team, remember?"

Before he could respond, she rose to her feet and sashayed to the bed, giving the swing of her hips an extra little sway.

He followed right behind her. "Minx."

When she turned in surprise, he covered her mouth with his.

This was the kiss he'd longed to give when she'd won the race. Wild and untamed, sweet and celebratory, possessive and demanding. A kiss that acknowledged the win but was not yet done conquering. A kiss that claimed her as his own.

It wasn't enough. He lowered his mouth to her neck, to the curve of her shoulder, to her breast.

The gasp of pleasure that escaped her

throat was nearly his undoing. As if her knees had weakened at his touch. She seated herself unsteadily on the edge of the mattress and reached for him.

It was the welcome he'd been waiting for.

Without taking his mouth from her breast, his fingers found the wet heat between her thighs. A delicious rhythm unfurled: suckling, stroking, suckling, stroking, until she arched her spine and cried out as the spasms took her.

When she collapsed backward against the mattress, he did not climb atop her. Instead he sank to one knee and placed his mouth where his fingers had been. In no time at all, his tongue coaxed her back toward the peak.

"Now," she whispered, tugging him toward her. "I want all of you."

He lifted his head from between her thighs with one last, lingering lick. "I can't."

She jerked her head up from the bed. "What?"

"As much as I would dearly love to position myself between your legs and thrust until we can't see straight, I can't hold myself up with one arm and I don't want to crush you."

"But…" She blushed.

"Fortunately, there's another way." He lowered himself onto the bed beside her and gave her a wicked smile. "If you want to ravish me, you'll have to do it yourself."

Her eyes lit up. "Can I taste you like you tasted me?"

The swollen member jutted up between his legs.

"Straddle my hips," he said hoarsely, "and ride."

She knelt over him, her legs straddling his. But then she lowered her head, her soft hair falling to his taut stomach, hiding her lips from view. She immediately placed her mouth about his member and gave an experimental lick.

Every muscle in his body twitched at once.

"Felicity..." he growled.

She ignored the warning and sucked instead, just as he had done to her breast.

He sucked in a tortured gasp of air, unable to think from the rush of pleasure.

"Felicity," he rasped hoarsely, reaching for her hand. "For the love of all that's holy... *Ride.*"

After a final lick of his member, she then positioned herself so that it nudged her opening.

Inch by inch, she began to lower herself onto him. He lifted his good hand to where their bodies joined. His thumb made lazy little circles that caused her to hitch her breath as the growing slickness quickly seated their bodies together.

"Am I hurting you?" he asked quietly.

"No." Her passion-drugged eyes lifted to his. "Am I hurting *you?*"

"If you stop, I'll die."

"I never want to stop." She moved her hips, rocking against him, lifting and lowering.

The muscles in his legs tightened as he strained to keep from release until she'd found hers, too. With the pad of his thumb, he coaxed her back to the precipice to join him.

"Giles," she gasped.

That was all she had time to say before her muscles contracted around him. When she caught her breath, she asked, "Are you—"

"Right now," he growled, hauling her off of him with his good arm and covering his bucking hips with the bedclothes.

He curled himself about her, his good arm crossing possessively over her chest and stomach.

And then, if he wasn't mistaken, a tiny snore escaped her lips.

He pressed a kiss to her hair and gave himself over to sleep. When next he opened his eyes, the angle of the sun indicated hours had passed. Mid-morning had become afternoon. If he didn't act fast, the day would be gone… and so would Felicity.

Her brother had already indicated he would refuse consent to the match. But Giles didn't give a damn what the Duke of Colehaven wished. Giles wanted to marry Felicity. Her feelings were the only ones that mattered.

"Are you awake?" he murmured into her hair.

She nodded. "But I'm not ready to leave this bed."

He hoped she never would.

Now that he'd committed to pursuing this path, he was at a loss as to what the right words were. What was the proper post-coital procedure to broach the topic of wedding someone you had never officially entered courtship with?

"Felicity," he began tentatively. "I really like you."

Smiling, she turned so that their foreheads touched. "I like you, too."

"Let's get married," he blurted.

There. The words were out. They had an impact, all right.

Just not the intended one.

He wasn't sure what stung worse: her involuntary wince at the idea, or the *oh god what do I do now* terror in her eyes.

"If you're uninterested, just say so," he said stiffly. "Put me out of my misery."

"I'm extremely interested," she said. "Close to obsession, really. You're all I ever think about. But… I can't."

Elation at her reciprocated interest crashed into the brick wall of rejection.

He tried to understand. "We just—"

"I know." She looked tortured. "But no one else has to. Just like I can't tell anyone

I wear lads' clothing and work on carriages."

"You told me," he pointed out. "I like it. I like *you*. This is love. If you feel the same, let's make it last forever."

"It's not that simple." She bit her lip, her brown eyes pained. "Yesterday, I... That is, Lord Raymore..."

Giles sprang upright, wounded arm be damned.

"You're betrothed to someone else?" he burst out in shock and disbelief.

"Not yet," she said at once, then lowered her gaze. "But that's the path I'm on. It's... not about *you*..."

"Then why are you *here?*" he demanded. "In my house. In my bed."

Her eyes filled with grief. "Giles..."

"Do you love him?" he asked quietly.

"I love *you*," she answered. Her eyes begged for him to believe her.

But if true, it only made him hurt worse.

He backed away from the bed until his head touched the wall and there was nowhere else to go.

She had a better offer. A titled lord with piles of gold and a collection of fancy estates. And the blackguard was *nice*. How was he supposed to compete with that?

"Is that what you want?" he asked hoarsely.

Of course it was. She'd told him so a hundred times.

"Is it what you *still* want?" he corrected. "A man who meets your criteria, but doesn't hold your heart?"

"No," she answered brokenly. "Not at all, but it's the right thing to do. Even if he wasn't the best shot at raising funds to support impoverished children, I promised my brother I would make the highest match I could get, to a man he approved of. Cole was hoping for duchess and Raymore is only a marquess, but—"

"Only a marquess," Giles repeated, not bothering to hide his bitterness and hurt. "How will you suffer the ridicule?"

He'd meant to be sarcastic, but his razor-edged words only succeeded in wounding himself.

A marquess was an acceptable stand-in for a duke.

A coach smith was not.

He was the one who would cause her ridicule. *He* was the one whose company could never be endured in public.

He was the one she could live without.

"Giles…" Her eyes pleaded for understanding.

"If you change your mind, you know where to find me. And if you don't change your mind…" He gestured toward the door. "Don't come looking."

CHAPTER 15

Felicity slumped against the wall of the hackney cab and buried her face in her hands.

Keeping one's promise to one's brother was the honorable thing to do. Keeping one's vow to indigent children with no other hope was the *moral* thing to do.

Yet walking away from Giles hadn't felt like the right thing.

It had felt like losing everything.

Including her soul.

"Where to?" the driver asked.

"Grosvenor Square," she mumbled.

That wasn't what she wanted, either. There was nothing wrong with fighting for others. But sometimes, a woman had to fight for herself, too. Now that she'd tasted love, now that she knew what life with Giles might be like, how could she settle for anything less?

She couldn't. Nothing was worth giving up love.

Felicity lifted her tear-streaked face from her hands and gazed down at her trouser-clad thighs. This could be the last time she dressed like who she truly was… or the first day of a better life. A life where she didn't have to hide anymore. Where she could follow her passions, no matter what or who that might be.

If she went back to Giles now and begged for a second chance to get the answer right, he would always believe it was her marriage to him that ruined her standing in society and everything she wanted out of life.

Rubbish, of course. He was the best part of her. If it took losing her reputation to have him, then she'd do so first and openly, to prove choosing him was what *she* wanted, and that he wasn't ruining anything.

"Driver!" She banged on the wall. "I've changed my mind. The Haymarket, please."

He made the next turn.

She smoothed her trousers and smiled. Ladies weren't allowed in the Wicked Duke? Felicity was no lady. She would show everyone in London exactly what she thought of their rules, and prove to Cole that sometimes the "best" match wasn't made in Almack's, but in the heart.

"Haymarket," said the driver without pulling over to the side of the road.

There was nowhere to go. So many horses

and carriages filled the lanes around the Wicked Duke, there had barely been enough room to squeeze the hack into the mix.

Her legs trembled. Cole had always told her the tavern was *the* place to be after a big race, but she hadn't expected this many people would bear witness to the scandal she was about to cause.

Even better, she told herself as she flipped the driver a coin. By the time word reached Giles, she would be infamous. He would know she was choosing to be with him because she'd chosen to be *herself*.

She marched into the Wicked Duke with her hands in her trouser pockets and her head held high.

"F-felicity?" Lord Raymore spluttered in disbelief.

Her heart jumped at the unexpected encounter. But of course he was here. Everyone else was. And Raymore deserved as much as anyone to know exactly what sort of woman he'd almost proposed to. Let him count his blessings that he was finding out now.

"*Lady* Felicity?" blurted another of her brother's friends. "In *trousers?*"

"Lady Felicity in trousers!" A cheer went up and glasses clinked around the tavern as if they'd been waiting for the sister of a duke to walk through the door and cause the scandal of the season.

Her brother did not take up the cry. As he

turned toward her, his pale cheeks mottled alarmingly in disbelief.

The crowd fell to a hush, their attention rapt.

Chin up, she strode forward to face him.

He looked like he wished to throttle her. "What the devil do you think you're—"

"I don't want to be a marchioness," she blurted.

Cole opened his mouth.

"Or a duchess," she added. "Or a countess or a viscountess or any other '-ess.' I don't want to be 'a lady.' I want to be Felicity. After so many years of doing my best to blend with others, I've finally figured out who I truly am. *This* is me." She gestured at herself. "*This* is the sister you've known all your life. I've tried so hard to be someone else, but I can't bear to live a lie for the rest of my life. Even for you."

She prepared herself for the worst.

Her brother looked stricken. "I never wanted any of that for me. I wanted it for you."

"You're... not disappointed?" she stammered.

"I'm disappointed in *me*," Cole answered, his cheeks flushing with shame. "From the time you were small, I've made you think you had to live whatever life I orchestrated for you. From the little helper at my heels in the smithy, to some grandiose matron of the ton. I was trying so hard to give you everything *I* wanted you to have, that I never stopped to ask you what *you* wanted."

"I just wanted to make you proud," she mumbled.

It was all she had ever wanted. To matter. To be important. To be accepted for who she was.

"You *do* make me proud." He grasped her shoulders. "Felicity, there's no better sibling a man could have. You've been my brother, my sister, my best friend, my confidante… My constant companion since the day you were born. I owe the world to *you*. Not the other way around."

Her hands trembled.

"I wanted you to make a splendid match because *you* are splendid," he said softly. "I want you to have your best chance at happiness. That's all I've ever wanted."

She drew a shaky breath.

He touched his knuckle to her chin. "The most splendid match you can make is with the man who loves you and makes you happy. Nothing else matters, Felicity. I swear it. Go with your heart. It will never lead you wrong."

Before her eyes filled with tears in front of all these witnesses, she turned toward the door—and locked eyes with the only man she wanted.

He leaned against the far wall; his wounded arm tucked in a sling over his chest. The knuckles on his good hand were bruised now, too. Possibly due to the shiner currently empurpling one of Silas Wiltchurch's eyes.

"Am I interrupting?" she asked tentatively.

Giles lifted a shoulder. "I was showing this gentleman the exit."

"I'll do it!" Half a dozen men leaped to their feet at once to escort a sullen Wiltchurch to the door.

"Don't bother to come back," Cole called without bothering to look over his shoulder. "Your kind isn't welcome here."

Her heart caught.

Silas Wiltchurch, nephew to one of society's most powerful patronesses, was unwelcome.

Felicity could stay. Exactly how she was.

Now that she was here, how could she prove to Giles how much he meant?

"Is there a betting book?" she asked her brother.

He nodded, then frowned. "How many bad habits do you have?"

She ignored him and squared her shoulders.

"Giles Langford," she called out as she strode straight toward the man. "I challenge you to a carriage duel."

He narrowed his eyes as she drew closer. "What's a carriage duel?"

"A race in which the loser owes the winner a boon," she explained to the delight of the onlooking crowd. Several were already racing toward the betting book. "If I win, you marry Lady Felicity."

His arms were already reaching toward her. "And if I win?"

"You marry Lord Felix," she answered, lips twitching.

"Deal," was the last thing he said before his mouth slanted over hers and the tavern's whoops and wolf-whistles drowned out the pounding of their hearts.

This was what winning felt like.

One year later

"Are you certain this is straight?" Giles called down from atop the ladder propped in front of the smithy.

"It's perfect," came his wife's satisfied reply.

"I'm nailing now," he warned. "This is how it's going to look from this day forward."

"Or until there's another Langford," she answered with a teasing wink.

He stepped down from the ladder to admire the smithy's new *Langford & Langford* sign.

"Don't you think *Langford & Langford & Langford* would start to get repetitive?" he asked.

"Fair point," she said after a moment. "We should let the children decide if and how they'd like to be represented."

He swung her into his arms and gave his gorgeous wife a kiss full of promise.

"Don't start something we can't finish," she warned him. "I've barely half an hour to change clothes."

His wife was currently in trousers, her hair tied in a simple tail, her smile as wide as his own. She didn't look a lad *or* a lady. She looked like Felicity.

And there was no one Giles loved more.

"You're not off for a test drive?" he asked in surprise.

She shook her head. "Directors' meeting at the foundation."

"Directors can't wear trousers?" Giles teased.

"Low bodices raise more donations," she answered with a saucy wink, and turned for the door.

He grinned after her.

After the wedding, her brother and his wife had joined forces with her and Giles to start the charitable foundation she'd always dreamed of. As soon as there was an account to deposit funds into, all four of them made the case to a packed crowd at the Wicked Duke.

Giles might not possess a title or entailed estates, but he was one of the most popular men in the city. Between his celebrity and both tavern owners taking up the cry in their respective exclusive gentlemen's clubs, the foundation was off to a roaring start. In a little over a year, Felicity had a team of assistants, a detailed plan for disseminating food and clothing, and the money to start building a home for those who had nowhere else to go.

"Is there room for *Langford & Langford & Neighborhood Lads?*" asked one of his young helpers.

"*Langford & Langford & Neighborhood Lads & Lasses,*" corrected his younger sister with her arms crossed over her leather apron.

Giles squinted up at the sign. It did have a nice ring to it.

"Maybe," he said cheerfully and climbed back up the ladder. "Can one of you hand me the paintbrush?"

THE END

Love talking books with fellow readers?

Join the *Historical Romance Book Club* for prizes, books, and live chats with your favorite romance authors:
Facebook.com/groups/HistRomBookClub

Check out the *12 Dukes of Christmas* facebook group for giveaways and exclusive content:
Facebook.com/groups/DukesOfChristmas

Join the *Rogues to Riches* facebook group for insider info and first looks at future books in the series:
Facebook.com/groups/RoguesToRiches

Check out the *Dukes of War* facebook group for giveaways and exclusive content:
Facebook.com/groups/DukesOfWar

And check out the official website for sneak peeks and more:

www.EricaRidley.com/books

~

Don't forget your free book!

Sign up at http://ridley.vip for members-only exclusives, including advance notice of pre-orders, as well as contests, giveaways, freebies, and 99¢ deals!

ACKNOWLEDGMENTS

As always, I could not have written this book without the invaluable support of my critique partner, beta readers, and editors. Huge thanks go out to Darcy Burke, Rose Lerner, Erica Monroe, and Tracy Emro. You are the best!

Lastly, I want to thank the *Historical Romance Book Club* facebook group and my fabulous street team. Your enthusiasm makes the romance happen.

Thank you so much!

ABOUT THE AUTHOR

Erica Ridley is a *New York Times* and *USA Today* best-selling author of historical romance novels.

In the new *Rogues to Riches* historical romance series, Cinderella stories aren't just for princesses... Sigh-worthy Regency rogues sweep strong-willed young ladies into whirlwind rags-to-riches romance with rollicking adventure.

The popular *Dukes of War* series features roguish peers and dashing war heroes who return from battle only to be thrust into the splendor and madness of Regency England.

When not reading or writing romances, Erica can be found riding camels in Africa, zip-lining through rainforests in Central America, or getting hopelessly lost in the middle of Budapest.

~

Let's be friends! Find Erica on:
www.EricaRidley.com